Patrick Gale was born on the Isle of Wight. He spent his infancy at Wandsworth Prison, which his father governed, then grew up in Winchester before going to Oxford University. He now lives on ~ ⸢   ⸣f this country's best-loved r   are *A Perfectly Good Man*,   *Notes from an Exhibition*,   *called Winter*.

Praise for *Ease*:

'A quick-thinking book by an author who has something to say' *Guardian*

'Patrick Gale is among the great, unsung English novelists. Think Austen, Hardy, Murdoch. Remarkable' *Independent*

'A huge treat ... He is one of my favourite writers' Jane Green, *Daily Mail*

'Gale is a master at getting under the skins of his characters and revealing the undercurrents that drive apparently ordinary lives' *Mail on Sunday*

'A sleek and silky novel' *Boston Sunday Globe*

'*Ease* is a second novel by a young Briton whose gifts and insights are notable' *International Herald Tribune*

'Captivating. A novel that pleads to be read at a single sitting' *Publishers Weekly*

PATRICK GALE

EASE

TINDER
PRESS

First published in Great Britain by Abacus in 1986.

First published in this paperback edition in 2018 by Tinder Press
An imprint of HEADLINE PUBLISHING GROUP

1

Cataloguing in Publication Data is available from the British Library

ISBN 978 1 4722 5558 7

Typeset in Sabon 10.5/14.55 pt by Jouve (UK), Milton Keynes

Printed and bound in Great Britain by Clays Ltd, Elcograf S.p.A.

HEADLINE PUBLISHING GROUP
An Hachette UK Company
Carmelite House
50 Victoria Embankment
London EC4Y 0DZ

www.tinderpress.co.uk
www.headline.co.uk
www.hachette.co.uk

For dear Nick, with fond esteem
(Notting Hill, October 1984)

The compensation of a very early success
is a conviction that life is a romantic matter.
In the best sense one stays young.

F. Scott Fitzgerald, *The Crack-Up*

In her youth, such evenings alone with her three cherished contemporaries had been a rare indulgence; now that she approached her prime they formed the limping heart of her lame social round. Dinner was finished and a scent of dead candles hung, acrid, on the air. There was a lull in the truffle-weighted conversation, broken only by the sighing of the gas-fire and an occasional gurgle as steak was ushered into gut. She drained her brandy glass, set it on the rug and nestled back into her armchair. Standing at the bookcase behind her, Rick muttered as he flipped the pages in an album of press cuttings. From the chair on the other side of the mantelpiece, her Randy was staring at the fire, exhausted beyond the faintest expression. Their hostess's liberality had been extended as much to herself as her guests; Ginny lay sprawled on the sofa, mouth agape, flesh easing its too, too solidity through a ladder near the top of her tights. The hand that had been nursing a glass trailed onto the rug below her. With each deep breath her form slid a fraction further over the brink. She would tumble soon and then they could leave. Domina ran a hand through her hair and glanced across at Randy to bring him in on the joke. He was pretending not to have seen. Over the salmon, Ginny had paid him the compliment – characteristically barbed – that he didn't have the look of a live-in lover of eighteen years' standing. Domina glanced back to her schoolfriend and wondered that her company hadn't aged Rick faster than it had.

'Here we are,' said Rick suddenly. 'I knew I had it. June '66 . . . "The new Marlowe Society production of *As You Like It* is graced by a sprightly Rosalind in the person of Miss Fiona Templeton." There, I said it was her and not Gemma.'

The sudden voice woke his wife and precipitated her passage to the rug. Randy sprang forward and helped her back into a crash-landing position on the sofa. Domina stood.

'Is that the time? Rick, darling, I really think we should be . . .'

'Oh. Must you?' asked Rick.

'Well. Work and all that,' muttered Randy.

'Don't you bloody dare,' Ginny began, then subsided once more.

'Rick, you're sweet and it's been lovely.' Domina planted a kiss on his cheek. 'But we must let you both get to sleep.'

She walked out to the hall to retrieve her coat. The men followed her, Bronx and Windsor exchanging manly reassurances. She handed Randy his scarf. He had barely caught her eye since they left the table. Rick opened the door onto the Clifton pavement. A summer shower was falling.

'God, it's piddling down,' he said. 'Do you want to borrow an umbrella?'

'No. Honestly. It's only a bit of drizzle.'

'Yeah,' added Randy, 'it'd wake us up a bit.'

'No, go on. Take it. I'll drop round and pick it up tomorrow.' Rick pressed it on them. His novels were unreadable, but he was the soul of tact.

'Thanks,' Domina accepted. "'Night, Ginny. Lovely evening,' she called over Rick's shoulder, and they were alone in the rain.

Domina had hoped for a little flurry of amiable backbiting once they were out of earshot, but Randy was offering nothing. They walked half the familiar stretch between Royal York Crescent and The Paragon in silence, then he rapped her skull with one of the umbrella prongs.

'Ow,' she said.

'Sorry,' he said.

'That's OK,' she said, and they walked a little further. 'I know we've been living together so long that everyone assumes you're my husband not my lover,' she began at last, 'but I do think you might have sprung to my defence.'

'When?'

'When Ginny attacked me.'

'She didn't.'

'She did. She said my success had been too easy and that the comforts of my life were made manifest as a complacent, not to say unrelieved tone in my plays. I call that an attack. That analyst Rick's found her is a disaster. She needs a spell at a health farm; lots of raw food and exercise, no gin, and plenty of personal comments.'

They reached the half-moon of fanlights that was The Paragon. Randy leant against a lamp-post and pulled her to him, letting the umbrella slip aside.

'Aw, did she make my baby feel insecure, den?'

'Yes, she did. A little.' She smiled up at him. He started to kiss her but a fat raindrop slipped past her collar and onto her spine. She shuddered and broke away. 'Come on,' she said, 'let's get into the warm.'

She was irritated at her failure to match his youthful spontaneity. She had never been much taken with haystacks or railway carriages and this made her feel painfully sensible – like being unable to run with friends' children on the beach. Perhaps she could repair the mood once they were inside. She took the umbrella and, placing her arm in his, hurried for their front door. His arm dropped hers even before he had to reach for the key.

The house was dark. Domina shuddered.

'Boiler's gone out again,' said Randy and walked into his study.

'Are you going to work?' she asked, hanging up her coat.

'Yup.'

'Late?'

'Yup. Yup.'

She leaned against the hall wall, listening to the syrupy tick of the longcase clock and watching his back. He settled down at his desk and flicked on the Anglepoise. *Hymnals of Radical Insanity*: Smart, Blake, Cowper and co. He'd made up a bed in his study so that she could sleep through his irregular bouts of composition. It was a mess of twisted sheets.

'You don't want to come to bed now and get up early?' she tried.

'I'll get up early, but I'm gonna work now as well.' He didn't turn. She could go in and massage those shoulders but that would weaken her position. She stayed put.

'Randy, don't sulk.'

'Who's sulking?'

'You are.'

He turned, a battle won.

'Look, Domina.' That oh-so-rational tone. 'Today's the twenty-eighth. I promised Jonathan I'd get him a first draft by the eighth. That's less than two weeks and I'm less than two-thirds through. Be reasonable, OK?'

She walked forward and leaned in the doorway.

'I'm sorry. It was only a drop of rain running down my back.'

'What's that?' he said, peering at a sheet of manuscript.

'Nothing. I'll go and fix the boiler.'

He slipped on his headphones as she turned away. He'd worked to music ever since that gestalt therapy course at St Clare's. She had looked at the cassettes – tinkly Baroque stuff.

Twenty years ago she had leapt at him. Working-class heroes had been sexy, chic. In the years after Cambridge the common touch had been *de rigueur.* She had flaunted him to her parents' faces, delighting in their concern when she announced that they were 'co-habiting'. (*Sinful Living,* Queen's Theatre, Shaftesbury Ave, '66–'67.) She had never ceased to be amused at the speed with which their shared prosperity had caused the world to treat them as spouse and spouse. At first the spirit of rebellion, then a superstitious fear that the thrill would go, had kept them from the registry office door; now they remained single from rank apathy.

Domina descended the stairs to the basement kitchen. The offending boiler was boxed in below an airing cupboard. She crouched with a grunt, yanked open the door and peered at the instructions for relighting the pilot light. From upstairs came the tapping and spasmodic bleeps that would last well into the night and which would greet her when she rose in the morning to run a bath. There was always a chance that her bedside light would no sooner be out than footsteps on the stairs would herald a spectacularly tactile apology, but recent experience had shown it to be cruelly slim. She pressed button 2. There was a clank and a muffled, gaseous thud. Through the grimy glass she saw the steady tongues of fire.

She started back up the stairs and paused outside his study door. The tapping was fast and furious; he'd had an idea. She stooped to straighten the linen on his sofa bed, and to plump out his pillows. He didn't turn. When he rested briefly, she could hear a thin, rhythmic whisper from his headphones.

'Randy?' she said. There was no reaction. 'Doctor Herskewitz, I want your baby but we're running short of time.'

No reaction.

A variety of things had been left on the bottom step for carrying up later. She picked them up now. The latest edition of *Architectural Digest*, that carried a feature on the work they'd had done on the house. Proofs of last year's play, which French's were about to bring out. *Dread Myrmidon*. Two bars of soap. A packet of tampons. Toothpaste. Randy's favourite pair of Levi's that she'd been mending. The clatter of his typewriter followed her as she carried the armful to their room.

His last year's thesis, *The Broken Phrase*, which had shaken the literary establishment to the roots, had been on everybody's lips when she arrived at Cambridge for her first term. For a twenty-one-year-old, born and bred in the Bronx, to set forth a New Criticism and actually get published was no mean feat. The New Depression, however, and the arrival of middle-age on the horizon, had led to a need for security. The lure of a department headship, departmental funds, lecture tours, easy publication, had blunted his approach. The same axe but ground almost to the shaft.

She tossed the jeans on to his side of the bed, then sat at her dressing-table. She pulled open the drawer to put away the tampons. She paused halfway through shutting it again, to take out last month's pill cycle.

She had stopped taking the contraceptives over four weeks ago on impulse. She told herself she would tell Randy if he bothered to ask, but he hadn't. Nothing happened. She had been on the wretched things far too long – having an instinctive dislike of foreign bodies, rubber, coiled or other-wise. Filled with dread by stories of not so vestal brides who had been forced on to fertility drugs, she had visited Doctor Jameson last week. The tests had shown her to be a potential Ceres.

She sliced up the foil packet with some nail scissors and stuffed it into an empty soap box in the wastepaper basket. Poor Randy. Then she took up her hairbrush and ran it crossly over her scalp a few times. She undressed and walked over to draw the curtains. The rain had stopped and the sky was clear and spangled. Only half aware of the chill creeping over her skin, she stared down to the eerie pattern of orange lights that mapped out the deserted docklands far below.

Evenings with Rick and Ginny taught her a repeatedly forgotten lesson; the undiluted encounter encouraged fruit-less reminiscence, and always left her with the illusion that life had unwound with sickening rapidity. Conversation tended to circle around careers – careers in a vacuum without the trauma and the messy joys that attended them – reducing thirty-nine years to an ascending arc of achievement that was all too pat. It made her feel her age.

There was a sudden clatter of frenzied drumming from the converted hayloft over the garage. Seamus was home. Her lodger. Their lodger. Seamus was meant to be studying design at Bristol Poly but was suffering a crisis of faith. He played with an anarchic pop group.

She brushed teeth, washed face and climbed into bed with *Architectural Digest*. As she read the glowing terms in which the writer described 15, The Paragon, Clifton, and how its conversion so perfectly reflected the needs of literary critic, R.E. Herskewitz and playwright, Domina Feraldi (39), Domina sensed once too often a profound need for change.

2

She had passed Monday night in a favourite Bath hotel, simply for the hell of it. Now she had travelled up to Paddington first class, because it was a special occasion. Cases at her side beneath the departures board, she was grateful for the respite that luxury had granted her nerves. A man abandoned a trolley and Domina seized it. She heaved both cases on board, slung handbag and typewriter on top, and trundled off towards the newsagent's.

Five minutes later she was seated in a window of the restaurant, wrapping herself around a strong black coffee, a comforting chocolate croissant mutation, a *Times*, a *Standard* and a *Guardian*. She had travelled up with the last of the commuters and the first wave of mid-season salesgoers. The restaurant was fairly empty. A mid-morning lull. Across the aisle a Japanese child was picking exquisitely at a regulation sandwich. She raised brown eyes to Domina and smiled obediently. Her mother, in cream, murmured something at which her child pushed aside her plate, wiped her hands on a paper napkin, and trod a path to the Ladies.

Domina glanced over the headlines, then turned to the small ads and property sections of *The Times*. Exorbitant short lets. Unappealing flatshares. Areas far too desirable. She turned to the *Guardian*. There were no bedsits. She wanted the bedsit she had never had. She read curiously

through the flatshare column, and smiled that she was neither black, Buddhist, open brackets twenty-one close
brackets, or vegan. As the lesser and cream-clad Japanese
left their table, Domina turned to the tabloid. She had telephoned the Students' Union accommodation office the
previous afternoon, and they had recommended it as a
valuable source. She glanced at the pictures of a bomb inci-
dent, then wound her way through the cross-indexing to a
half-page of properties to let. She gleaned a supportive
horoscope on the way.

BAYSWATER, single bedsit in desirable position. Shared
bathroom and kitchen facilities.
Own fridge. Serviced. £28 p.w. inc. H W & Elec.

She encircled the telephone number and hurried to the
payphone.

The dial was grimy and the lists of dialling codes were
masked by a web of jotted numbers. A small white sticker
proclaimed: 'Penelope – New Exotic Model' and a Bayswater number. Domina had barely registered the numbers'
parity when she had to push in her ten pence.

'Hello? I'm ringing up about the ad in the *Standard* . . .
Yes, the bedsit. Has it gone? . . . It hasn't? Wonderful . . .
Of course. I'm at Paddington.' She did not bother to jot the
directions down. 'Sussex Gardens, Lancaster Gate and
along the Bayswater Road to the last turning before Queensway? Thanks . . . Oh yes. My name's Domina Tey. Mrs
Domina Tey . . . that's right. I'll get over as soon as I can.
Bye-bye.' Domina rang off, bought another cup of coffee
and returned jauntily to her table. She settled down to the

Guardian crossword, then slipped guiltily over to the one in *The Times*.

She had felt bad about leaving Randy a note. She would have talked to him about it but his adorable uncomprehending 'reasonableness' would have wet-squibbed her spontaneity. It might also have convinced her to stay at home. The adventure of a lifetime would have been diluted into a sensible weekend in Bath, or perhaps a planned, booked, and generally circumscribed trip overseas, *with* Randy and after he had finished the *grande oeuvre*. No thanks.

'Darling Randy', she had scribbled, fingers stiff with excitement, 'I won't be in for dinner for a few weeks but the freezer is well stocked. I've woken with complacency and menopause looming rather more than usual and have had to run away. *I'm not leaving you*, I'm simply going on a "visit to myself" for a bit. Sorry if this shocks but there we are. Communication not terribly easy at the moment 'cause of kookie Cowper. Know you'll understand. Please forward anything to me care of Des, and *do* write yourself. Secrecy of whereabouts vital to success of spiritual growth. Kiss Seamus for me, or pat his snare-drum or something.

Apologetic affec.

Mxxxxxxxx

P.S. Tell *Them* Mamma's fallen sick and I've rushed to the Tuscan bedside . . .'

3

The house was a late Victorian, quasi-Parisian pile propped between two self-important, diminutive hotels, the Inverness Plaza and the Kensington Towers. As Domina thanked the cabby for unloading her baggage she noted that it was one of the few non-commercial buildings in the row. One star. Two stars. B and B from £25 a night. The Metropole. The Britannia. Number 33 was blatantly ill-kempt, holding out staunchly against the tide of renovation. She stood outside the moss-flecked porch and looked up to some blood-red geranium that perched on the topmost window-sill. The place was perfect.

The ground-floor window trundled up in a swirl of net.

'You Mrs Tey?'

'Hello.'

'Come on in, love.'

Domina picked up her cases and swung them up the steps. A departing Pakistani handed her her typewriter with a smile.

'Oh. Thank you so much.'

'My pleasure.' He walked on, her eyes on his cheery back, and she found that if she stood on tiptoe she could see over the hedge on the Bayswater Road into the Gardens.

'Come in, love.' A plump creature with frizzed, reddish hair and a face like a dried dumpling. 'I'm Tilly. Tilly Widdowes.' They shook hands. 'Pleased to meet you.' Domina checked slightly at the frank statement of nicotine, but the woman had a winning smile. 'Here, give us that.' Tilly took a suitcase and heaved it across the threshold. Domina shut the door behind her and set down her case beside the first one. 'I'll show you the room first,' Tilly continued. 'No point hauling that lot up there if you don't fancy it much. Top floor, you see.'

'Sounds marvellous,' Domina beamed, deciding that Tilly's voice was trustworthy, and they started up.

The hall and staircase were dark and cool after the fuss and glare outside. Tilly concentrated her efforts on climbing. She tugged at the banister rail as she went and her breathing grew heavier. Behind her, Domina watched the cellulite-pocked skin of her upper arm as it clenched and relaxed, clenched and relaxed. There were touches of grandeur about them. Huge ornate doors that once led to a first-floor salon now opened on to a piece of landing and three small, modern counterparts. Stretches of elaborate stucco work on cornice and pelmet were broken by plasterboard and fluorescent tubing. Tilly kicked out at a new swing door as they passed it. It had a window of reinforced glass and said FIRE ESCAPE in white letters on a green background.

'Bloody fire doors,' she said. 'You can live as you like when a place is your own, but as soon as you start charging rent those effing inspectors come round. Fire doors, fireproofed panelling, escape signs. Costs a small fortune.'

'And they make it so institutional, don't they?' offered Domina.

'Right pain,' Tilly went on. 'You're the first person to ring up.'

'Really?'

'Yeah. Been looking long?'

'No. I only arrived this morning.'

'You're lucky. Some girls can look for weeks. Here we are. Not a stunning view, but it's quieter than the front.' She pushed open a door and stood back for her visitor.

'Oh, perfect,' Domina exclaimed, glad to be counted among the girls. A maid's room. Under the eaves, so the ceiling bent and was interesting. Fitted carpet. A bed. An armchair. A chair and table. A miniature fridge. A gas fire with a meter. A wardrobe. Domina opened the little white desk and found a sink. The lid swung back against the wall to bring the mirror on its underside into view.

'You can keep coffee and tea and things on the shelves under there,' Tilly informed her, 'but there's a shelf in the larder for you downstairs, too. Kettle on the landing. And a hoover for when Mrs Moorhouse doesn't do her bit.'

'Perfect,' repeated Domina. She looked out of the window. Not a conventional 'view' certainly, not Kensington Gardens or clean creamy porches, but she could peer down into the courtyards below through the network of washing lines and pulleys. There was a broad windowsill for plants, and she could look over the chimney pots to the red insanity of the Coburg Hotel roof. She turned with a laugh in her voice. 'It's great. Yes, please.'

'Thank God for that. I couldn't face tramping up those stairs too often in one day. Right, love, come on down and we can have a nice drink and a chat. Settle you in.' She banged the door next to Domina's as they set off down again. 'That's Quintus, your neighbour. Nice boy. Very

14

quiet, though.' She looked over her nose, 'Very religious and correct and all that.'

'How many others are there here?'

'Twenty all told. They come and go. Quite a few travellers, salesmen and that; they use it as a base to come back to. Then there's Quin – he's been here two years now, and Thierry, he's French by the way, he's been here a year.'

'All men?'

'Mostly. There's Avril though, on the first floor with the balcony, she's a lady writer, and Penny the actress, ever so pretty she is, and hard as they come. Girls don't go in for bedsits as much as boys, though. I think they prefer to find a flat and share with friends.'

They arrived back in the hall and Tilly led her new boarder into her flat off the hall. The main room was ruled by a vast black leather sofa – a four-seater – against one wall, and an imposing television – thirty-inch screen with doors – on the other side. A long-haired dachshund was lying on the sofa, her head drooping over the edge. She raised her eyebrows as they entered and began to growl, curling her lips.

'Shut up, you old bag; friends,' Tilly silenced her. 'Don't mind dogs, do you? That there's Grace. Used to belong to my mother-in-law, but she passed away and I just couldn't have her put down. Filthy temper. I reckon she's possessed. Make yourself at home. She never bites.'

Domina lowered herself as innocuously as possible into the far end of the sofa and bared her teeth at Grace. She held out a hand for the dog to sniff and roused another round of protest.

'Grace, shut it,' Tilly snapped, spinning round on her with lips tight and a finger raised. Grace shut it and, relenting, sniffed the proffered fingers. Then she waddled shakily across the leather cushions and sniffed Domina's skirt before sinking her head on to her thigh.

'There,' said Tilly, 'just like her old mistress – a right cow, but meek as you please once you let her know who's boss. What'll it be?' Tilly opened a drinks cabinet that had been masquerading as a chest of drawers. A light came on inside. It was full.

'Gin and tonic, please,' said Domina, who had been dreading milky coffee.

'Ice and lemon, love?'

'Lovely, I mean, yes please.' Domina was disturbed at the way the animal's eyes were gazing, restive, up at her. Its posture was unnaturally twisted. Gingerly she stroked its brow. As if at a sign, Grace withdrew her head, shifted her posture, and curled up in sleep at her side. 'Thanks. Have you lived here long?' asked Domina, taking her glass.

'All my life,' said Tilly, sitting at the other end of the sofa with a large Scotch. 'Born in the basement. That was a separate flat in them days. Dad ran a funeral parlour down Westbourne Park Grove. My old man was his apprentice and Dad bought us the upstairs here as a wedding present. It was in a god-awful state then. Been empty for years. Roof needing re-tiling, paintwork falling to bits. When Roy passed over five years back, that's my old man, I sold the business and used some of the cash to do the roof and stick in carpets and extra baths and that. Effing goldmine, now the area's up and coming. Shame I'm not still young enough to make the most of it, know what I mean?' Tilly let out a wheezy laugh. Domina smiled indulgently, they both sipped their drinks, then Tilly resumed, 'Where d'you come from then, er, Miss . . . ?'

'Domina, and actually it's Mrs.'

'Domina.'

'Durham,' Domina improvised. 'My late husband was a canon of the cathedral there. I taught in the choir school. English and French. But I need a change. I've no children or any relations to speak of, so I thought I'd come down here and try to find a flat and a new job. I grew up in London, in fact.'

'Oh yeah?'

'Yes. In Wandsworth. My father was the assistant governor of the prison.' Domina took a gulp of g and t. She was excited by the developing lie. This was as good as having one's hair done. 'Yes, I lived down here till I was nineteen, then I went up to Durham to go to university and that's where I met Paul, my husband.'

'Pass over recently, did he?'

'Just over a year ago.'

'I'm sorry.'

'Not at all. He was very sick. Hodgkin's disease. A merciful release, really.'

'D'your mum and dad still live here?'

'No. They retired to the Continent. My mother's half Italian you see, and she owns a house in Tuscany. They're very happy there.' A half-truth, this, to give the fiction a backbone. 'Did you *enjoy* working in an undertakers?'

'Great business.'

'I've never understood how people could. Didn't it ever upset you?'

'Oh yeah. To start with. Scared the arse off you, pardon me, at first. The first thing to hit you is the smell. Ever been in a basket workshop?'

'No. But I used to learn basketry and chair-weaving at evening classes.'

'Smells like that, but worse. Like when you wet the cane to make it all soft and there's the sweet, dusty smell. It's the fluids. When someone dies you think they've just stopped, like a car, but they don't. Specially if they died on a full stomach.'

'The hair and the toe-nails . . . ?'

'That's nothing. It's the wind that's dreadful. My first day in there, this man rang up and said he wanted to bring his sister to see his old girl laid out, like, and would we get her ready. Well they always need a good wash – wetting themselves, and worse, you see, like great grey babies they are. So Dad said, find her a dress. Find her a dress, he says, give her a wash and brush-up and slap a bit of lippy on her. You know. Make the old dear look a bit, well, life-like. 'Cause it's a terrible shock for people otherwise. Well anyway, she wasn't old at all, really, only about forty-two. Cancer, I think it was, but she was quite sweet looking and I wasn't scared or anything. So, I got a bowl of soapy water and a sponge and that, and started cleaning her up a bit, on the trolley like. Well, it was all hunky-dory till I tried to do her back. You see, if they die at home and get arranged by family, who don't know any better, it's OK because their insides get pushed around a bit and the, well, the wind and that,' Tilly made a face to show that they were women of the world together and Domina was touched by the confidence, 'the wind and that can get let out. But this old dear had gone in hospital and they're so bloody careful there. You know. She dies on a bed, and they lift her ever so careful on to a stretcher trolley, then slide her ever so careful into a placky bag for the likes of Dad to pick up in the morning. Well anyway, I takes her by the shoulders and heaves her up, to get her sitting up like, so's I can reach her back and the nape of her neck to wash off the sweat, and I swear to God, Domina, she let out a sigh!'

'God!' gasped Domina, enthralled.

''Course it wasn't really her, I mean it was just all the farts and burps and that sliding out at last through her voice box, but I screamed. God, how I screamed. It was so embarrassing. I just dropped her like a ton of bricks and shrieked, "Dad, Dad, she's alive, she's alive!" It's stupid, really, when you think about it, because you should be happy if someone came back to life and that. But all you can think, when you're standing in one of those places, is how much you don't want to see them move. It's like they're not the same, because they've been a corpse.'

'There's one thing I've always wanted to know,' said Domina, 'and that's what exactly *happens* in a crematorium.'

'No one ever told you?'

'Never.'

So, delighted to have a fascinated audience, Tilly told her the secrets of her old trade: the ins and outs of embalming fluid, the bags of neglected still-born babies that no one wants to deal with, and the way that corpses seem to sit bolt upright in the furnace for the seconds before they crumple into ash and bone. Then she showed Domina the bathrooms and the communal kitchen. The idiosyncrasies of the elderly twin-tub were outlined. A label with her name on was fixed to 'her' shelf in the larder. Keys were handed over, and a smart new rent book. Twenty-eight pounds a week including electricity, hot water, and a daily char. Domina paid her deposit of a month's rent, and went upstairs to unpack. Then, having made her bed with her own sheets, and christened the room with a few squirts of scent, she set off in search of a new image.

4

As Virginia was forever pointing out in her inebriated slurs, Domina ran on well-oiled rails. Her father had inherited his father's thriving publishing house, Pharos Company. This concern had come into being in an uncommercial, gentlemanly fashion, to print the ungentlemanly and equally uncommercial outpourings of the interbellum literary pride of which he was an adoptive cub. As the texts in his sway progressed from being wrapped in brown paper or displayed on only the more avant-garde occasional tables to being well-thumbed by back-packing Americans and religiously dissected during A-levels, Pharos Company had become synonymous with the best of modern English verse and with the less-readable of modern English prose. (It had been thanks to a personal introduction to her father that Rick, Ginny's husband, had first challenged the novel-reading public.)

Quietly rich, Jacoby Tey was an aesthete of the old school. In addition to his father's publishing house, he had inherited a Lutyens 'manor' in the South Downs. His wife, Isobella, was the daughter of a Tuscan count. ('Two-a-penny, *cara*,' she would say, 'but the surnames are so good for cheques.') The only child in a house where the lowliest soap dish was a thing of beauty, Domina had slept in a nursery decorated in her father's childhood by Dora

Carrington and friends. Isobella was a devout Catholic, he was semi-lapsed.

Once Domina's education was complete, the couple saw fit to separate. A divorce was out of the question on her part, and tactfully unrequested on his. His infidelities had begun soon after their child's conception and centred around budding authoresses and the London flat. Isobella would stay in the country with the baby and the dogs, passive, knowing, accepting, inviting said authoresses over for gracious weekends. Hers was a passivity Domina had failed to understand – until recently. The dogs had long since died, as had father, all but a generous clutch of shares in the company had been sold, and Isobella now lived with her philosophical half-sister, Juliana-Costanza, in her family's villa. When Domina had last visited her there, in the hills near San Giminiano, she had claimed to have loved Jacoby as much in the lecherous dotage preceding his death as she had always done. She opined that they lived apart because it was more practical that way, that she didn't want to make his girlfriends nervous. Her presence, if only chastely, as a handbag or a waft of good scent, would have required too much explanation.

From her arrival, Domina had been a piece of the house collection. Jacoby dressed her in frocks of unworldly charm, and had her painted, sculpted, photographed and filmed in each phase of her development. Isobella had her baptized, confirmed, heard her catechism and prayers and taught her Latin and Italian. In due course, at the time when the paternal indiscretions were growing too exhausting to mask, Domina was sent to board at a highly-respected convent school a-flutter with genuflecting debs. Crushes ensued: on nuns, on Crashawe, on the Mother Superior, on Sister Charity (games), on Saint Sebastian. The standard of secular education at Saint Mary's, Clanworth was superior; any efforts on the spiritual side were without great effect. Religion had always been bound up, in Domina's mind, with aesthetics. Charity, mystery and revelation were less essential than a sense of rightness, akin to knowing the proper vase for a lily or sensing that plovers' eggs were pleasing enough to need no further garnish than a piece of good crystal in which to cluster.

Her inheritance was not solely in pelf. Isobella's ear for voices, her ability to pin down characters and mimic with cruel precision was handed on. In looks, the daughter harked back to Jacoby, with a long, classical body – but too kind, even cherubic a face. Domina's appearance was modish enough in the mid-sixties, when women had to have Oxfam builds and soft, pearly-lipped faces, but it was unlikely to mature as superbly as her mother's Milan-coutured one. Her ear for good English came from exposure to her father's conversation. Even with his temper roused, his cadences had been perfect. His vocabulary had been vast. He gave her the two-volume Oxford dictionary for her thirteenth birthday and she had learnt to read it for the sheer pleasure of tracking down unfamiliar words, then daring to ease them into her talk. Less a tease at school than a merciless slanderer, she could be counted on to provide the sharpest account of any event. Other fourteen-year-olds never said words like 'lubricious' or 'obesity', contenting themselves with 'randy' or 'fat'; thus she distinguished herself, aroused a certain awe, raised laughs and, through the venom of her enmity, many friends.

It was only when first auditioned for a school play that a weakness was made manifest. Off-stage, Domina was graceful and well-spoken, but with a bowdlerized *As You Like It* in her sweaty paw, she had lurched around like a new-born calf and her voice had dribbled into her copy. Ever astute, Sister Annunciata (English) had perceived that Mina's words had to be her own. She knew she had written many trifles for home consumption. Making no promises, she had suggested she write an adaptation of a favourite book for the stage. *The Rose and the Ring* took the best part of a summer holiday to write. Excellent O-level results fired Domina to persevere. Her mother had delighted in taking her seriously and would dismiss her to the summer-house after breakfast, disturbing her only to bring out jugs of lemonade, a plate of sandwiches, or to call her out to tea on the lawn. In the evening Isobella would act as secretary, and type out the day's work, a fidgeting Domina at her elbow. The words were largely Thackeray's own, but the exercise taught the girl the foundations of stagecraft. At her father's suggestion, she had taken as models the family editions of Galsworthy, Shaw and Barrie. Thackeray's subversive whimsy was consequently buttoned into the confines of a well-made play, but for this very reason the nuns could find no objection to staging the thing as a Christmas play the following term.

A-levels followed, and Oxbridge. Domina won a scholarship to Girton and was sent on a trip to Europe as congratulatory preparation: Paris, Venice, Florence, Rome, Athens, then back to Sussex and the Reading List. At the convent they had studied little beyond the set authors of the syllabus. Faced with the sum total of English erudition outlined on three crisp sheets, Domina panicked and read her way through three and a bit centuries before arriving at Cambridge that autumn with little to show for her effort, beyond the fact that she had done so.

Domina's parents were not religious, they were Catholic. Religious parents watch over their offspring's soul: Catholic ones give it a Catholic education. The forms were observed. Rosaries, crucifixes, an annunciation by a query-pupil of Duccio hung in the dining room, lots of pretty nuns, her great-grandmother's first communion dress, a painting of her standing in the thing clutching Debrett's because the only Bible around was quite the wrong colour, and a deep and utter vacancy where sex education might have been. There was sex, certainly. Sex bubbled in the paths of the growing girl. She had sat with her dolls in the summer-house, gravely watching her father suck the buttons of Tamasin Boyce's slowly opening blouse. She had held solemn discussions with callow youths on the subject of women's liberation and the aesthetic influence of the Virgin Birth. She had pottered in and out of the studio where some naked friends of Jacoby's were posing for a Modernist sculpture of Diana and Endymion. When it came to what to do and how to avoid subsequent compromising disclosures, however, Domina had only inexplicable gestures and no knowledge upon which to rely. Whatever the state of their souls, Nanda Brookenham and poor knowing Daisy retained the physical vestige of their honour. At the end of her first Freshers' party, with three and a bit centuries of verse and prose, a strong line in arch small talk, and enough fashionable names for dropping to break a man's feet, Domina found herself in a dark room in King's, under a rather drunk young man with a spotty back. Some weeks later she found he had left her with more than the unlovely recollection.

She wandered around for a few days, aiming at a sense of sin and falling wide of the proper mark, then paid a visit to a man in Ipswich whose anonymous services were advertised on slips of card torn within days from the college noticeboards. The abortion had been short and thoroughly unpleasant, not least in the equanimity with which she discovered it could be faced. No one, not even Randy, had ever been told. Enlightenment ensued; with it, a discovery that she could write wittily about every facet of human life and not just every but one. With it also came a progression of increasingly interesting young men which culminated in one Randy Herskewitz. Champion of student rights and proletariat intelligentsia, he was incidentally the best thing thought up for bed since breakfast.

5

They first met in the Arts Theatre Ladies. Domina was suffering from cystitis and had to leave Randy in the auditorium and limp out before the first half was quite over. It was the première of her Footlights revue, the first to be written by a single author, and they were loving it. She wanted to sit and hold Randy's big hand and bask in the laughter, but her kidneys possessed less sense of occasion. She hurried, near cross-legged, to the Ladies, locked herself in a cubicle, sat down and sighed.

'Congratulations,' someone called out.

Domina had glimpsed someone sitting on a ledge by the wash-basins as she ran in. She called up at the gap over the door:

'Thanks.'

'It was you that wrote the thing, wasn't it?'

'That's right.'

'So good it makes me sick. Congratulations, as I say.'

'Thanks again. How did you know it was me?'

'I got here early and asked the director to point you out – what'sername, "Virginia Bingham".' The voice slowed up as it read out Ginny's name from a programme. 'Next half's better, though,' it continued.

The discrepancy between the occasion's joy and the person's lugubrious tone made Domina smile as she readjusted her frock and opened the door. She grinned as she walked over to join her at the basins, and started to wash her hands. Black, pudding-basin hair, head like a potato, crumpled, antiquated dress in blue satin.

'How d'you know?' asked Domina.

An ashtray was spilling at the woman's side.

'I've got a script. Cambridge actors make me throw – used to do props for the Marlowe Society – so I went backstage as soon as I'd heard enough, and got an ASM to flog me his script.'

'What?' Domina laughed.

'Fiver. Get it off him after the show. It could be your first earnings.'

Domina dried her hands.

'The actors are really quite good, you know,' she said. 'Jill St Clair's great.'

'Hate actors.' She sucked fiercely on the last inch of a cigarette, then crushed it in the ashtray. 'Want an agent?'

'An agent?'

'Yes. You're very good. Makes me sick, as I say. I'm an agent. I keep you in work, get you the best deals: you keep me in Woodies – say eight per cent – and give me the push if you're not happy after six months.'

Her frankness appealed. Domina knew all about agents from her father, but felt incapable of snubbing this one. This fat, funny one, chain-smoking Woodbines in a ladies' lavatory. She hesitated:

'Look. I don't . . .'

'Bristol Old Vic in August, Royal Court first week in September – if they like your stuff, which I know they will. I've got the backing, the goodwill and eight days left to find someone new.' She slapped the dog-eared script with the back of her hand. 'You fit the bill.' She grinned. Domina saw a gold tooth and was lost.

'OK. I can't think straight now, obviously, and I've got to get back in there and see what they're doing.'

'You can choose an assistant director and sit in on auditions.'

'Oh come on. I'm really interested and excited and ... give me your number. I'll call you tomorrow morning. Are you up for the night?'

'With my old tutor out at Kingston. I'm here till about three tomorrow.'

'Great. Let's have lunch.'

'026-9959.'

'026-9959.' Domina murmured as she scribbled in her programme.

'Des Turner. Des as in Desiree as in pink-skinned potato.'

The lucky break would undoubtedly have come without Des's help. Given her father's contacts, Domina knew that luck was scarcely involved. Her motive was a combination of a half-articulated desire to prove her professional independence from Pharos Company, and a long-standing talismanic attitude to atonement. From the first pretty dress and school fees envelope, Domina had felt an obligation to reciprocate good deed for felicity; a childish watercolour for a dress, a poem or a flower arrangement to ease her discomfort over the fees, gifts for others on her birthdays. As the blessings of fate grew in moment, so her grateful expiations took increasingly long-term and human forms. The success of the first play found Ginny the post of assistant director in the London transfer and took Domina on an overdue visit to her mother; that of the award-winning second saw an aberrant spate of church-going, confessions and all; that of the latest, which had won her a coveted prize, is driving her to dedicate all profits to an obscure RAF orphanage. The acclaim that greeted her revue, a revue that transferred to the West End for an unprecedented student run, was honoured by the adoption of Dr Desiree Turner as her literary agent.

Des still wore her hair like Henry V, but now it was streaked with silver. Her office was still a seedy room over Gloucester Road tube station, but she could now afford to pay an assistant reader-cum-typist. She specialized in playwrights and screenplay writers and now had several successes on her books, but Domina had remained her number one.

Her hands full of glossy carrier bags, Domina climbed the familiar greasy stair-carpet past the flatshare agency on the first floor and the nurse employment agency on the second and reached the door proclaiming:

'D.B. Turner BA. PhD.
Literary Agent'

where she dropped her bags and rang the bell. The PhD was on heroic verse drama of the nineteenth century, or something equally unlikely.

In the course of the lunch that Domina had bought her the next day in Cambridge and in the course of numerous ones she had bought her since, it had emerged that Des should have been a don at Newnham or an aggressively cerebral novelist, had tried to be both and had failed through a debility of *amour propre*. The latter prevented her from finishing any creative or academic venture, however promising its beginning. The PhD had only been completed because the disastrous love affair of the moment happened to be her supervisor. Domina's welling pity tended to dry at source on the reflection that by some mystery of fate and animal magnetism, Desiree Turner had never been without a lover of some description as long as they had known each other. To be sure, these shadowy figures were invariably problematical, traumatic even, but a failure is somehow less of a failure when she gets her oats.

Des opened the door, releasing a gust of Woodbine and Chianti. 'Oh my God, look who it isn't! You've had your hair cut somewhere absurdly expensive and you've been wasting money in King's Road and now you're going to sit down and tell me what in Christ's name is going on.' She picked up a few bags as she talked, and waddled ahead of Domina through the nicotinic haze to her desk. 'Paulette's getting married on Saturday, so we're getting pissed to help her forget.'

Paulette smirked at her desk. 'Oh, I'm ever so sorry to be leaving, you know,' she said, with a giggle. 'Would you like a glass, Ms Tey?'

'No thanks, Paulette. Actually, could I have some coffee?'

''Course. I'll get it straight away. Milk and one sugar, do you?'

'No sugar, thanks. I'm trying to cut down.' As Paulette meandered into the corridor that served as a kitchen, Domina sank into a chair opposite Des and called after her, 'Congratulations. What's the lucky man's name?'

'Geoff. We've been going steady for four years now, and as it's a leap year I waited till the special day came along and I thought, why not, so I popped the question.' She giggled again.

'Good for you.' Domina smiled across at Des. 'Shame to have to lose her so soon,' she consoled in a weighted undertone.

'Yeah,' mumbled Des, but gave the genuine reply by a heartfelt grimace and a loose flapping of the hand that wasn't clutching her Woodbine. 'Sure you don't want a drink?' she went on.

'No. Promise. I'm not very good at red wine without food.'

'Gives me gut rot too, but I must be past caring.'

Paulette returned and set down a steaming, chipped mugful for their guest. 'Milk and no sugar. Now I must be off or I'll miss the butchers.' She drained her glass with a dribbly grin, threw a magazine into her bag and headed for the door. 'I'll post the letters on my way, Des, OK? See you tomorrow. 'Bye.'

''Bye,' they both replied, and waited for the shutting of the door to relax them.

'Now,' said Des, 'first things first. Here's your mail.' She opened the top drawer and took out two bundles and slid them across her blotter to Domina. ' "Domina Feraldi", that's your fan mail, and there, "Ms Domina Tey", is your private correspondence.' Domina had written under her mother's surname from the start – 'Domina Tey' had always sounded like a clause from the Tridentine mass. 'Why the latter is being forwarded to me is what I want to know,' Des continued.

32

'I've run away, that's all.'

'Have you left him, then?'

'Not *left*, just left. He knows I'm coming back.'

'But *why*? You adore him. Don't you?'

'Yes, I know. It's simply that I was getting worried about my work.'

'But working at home must be so easy. You've a comfortable house, peace and quiet, loads of neurotic and over-aware neighbours to give you material. Did you argue?'

A train plunged beneath the office and rattled the windows. Domina waited for it to pass.

'No. Nothing like that. It's not really to do with him. It's just that ... well ... no, it is slightly to do with him.'

'Thought so.'

'But he hasn't done anything wrong. It's only that having him there all the time, worrying about his new book, beavering away in the study ... I mean ... I always find time for him when *I'm* working and ... well ... his being so preoccupied makes me feel rather small. And the others have been setting me thinking too, dropping heavy hints that it's all getting a bit safe and samey.'

'Virginia Bingham is a poisonous old soak. I don't know why you ...'

'Who said anything about Ginny?'

'She's the only badly insecure friend you've got.' Des stubbed out her Woodbine and burrowed in her bag for another packet. As she looked up and caught the fond grin in her client's eyes she grunted, 'Well, the only one in Clifton. Anyway, I'm a professional associate, which doesn't count.'

'OK, so Ginny's been foul, but she's also quite right.

Home is too secure. I'm running out of material and having Randy doing a Susan Sontag impersonation doesn't make it any easier to watch my increasing lack of intellectual or emotional gristle. My stuff's getting wordy and predictable.'

'Well, no . . . I—'

'Don't protect me. Any fool knows that there's a limit to the number of plots you can weave around menopausal lecturers and novelists.'

'You haven't run out of them yet.'

'But you admit that that's all I've been writing about.'

'What the hell? People love it. You're answering a chronic need among the discerning . . .'

' . . . *Guardian*-reading.'

' . . . *Guardian*-reading, professional-oblique-arty masses. Good for you. Long may you reign. And God help me if you start writing sub-Strindberg.'

'But Des.'

'What?'

'I think I'm getting bored.'

Desiree took a deep drag as she mulled this one over.

'Where are you staying?' Perfect tactic: Domina brightened up.

'Oh God, it's such fun! All my teens I yearned to be able to live in total squalor in a bedsit somewhere.'

'Virginia Woolf phase – I remember it well.'

'Yes . . . living in squalor, with a geranium on the windowsill and nothing to eat but coffee and digestives, with a typewriter and a houseful of peculiar little men.'

'And an eccentric landlady, who gives you material for short stories which you send in to a hand-printed quarterly somewhere off Tottenham Court Road.'

'Exactly. And I've done it.'

'What?'

'I'm living in a top-floor bedsit by Queensway, with no view, in a house full of odd little men and an old bag downstairs who used to be a mortician.'

'What now?'

'I wait. I've got the Olivetti. If anything stirs, I'll get tapping. It has to be better than pouring gin down Ginny's gullet and taking Randy pots of tea.'

'Does he know where you are?'

'No, and I've explained to him that he's got to humour me in my hour of need and not try to find out. He can forward all the mail to you and you can forward it on to me.'

'All sounds a bit Marie Antoinettish to me, but OK. If you think it'll help.'

'Good girl.'

Des paused, then asked, 'Are you certain there's nothing badly wrong that you haven't told me?'

'Yes, quite certain, Eeyore.'

'Good,' said Des, pulling a fat brown envelope from a wire tray and poising a severely mauled biro above it. 'Presumably you're living under some ridiculous pseudonym, in case any of the little men sees your name in *Time Out*?' she said, doggedly humouring.

'No. Just Tey – *Time Out* only lists me as Feraldi – but here I'm Mrs Tey.'

'Divorced botanist?'

'Not quite. Widowed schoolteacher from Durham. Poor dear Paul was a canon there until he died recently from something mercifully quick.'

'Kids?'

'We haven't got onto that yet.' Domina faltered. Des was bending over to empty the laden ashtray and did not see her flinch. As she sat up again, Domina caught her eye and laughed, 'I think I'm probably barren. Anyway, I'm down here flat-hunting and looking for a new post.'

'And/or hubby.'

'Of course. Someone settled and mature. Perhaps a professional widower with two children in their late teens and a rambling house on Clapham Common.'

'Write about it.'

'Oh, I couldn't.'

'Why not? It makes a change from lecturers and novelists, and it's too absurd to get mistaken for the truth. Anyone else know where you are?'

'Not a soul, and you're only to give it away in a case of dire emergency.'

Des yawned widely as she said, 'And presumably, in Virginia's case, only in a bad attack of impending death.'

6

The Paragon
Clifton
Bristol 8
Avon

So you've gone. You breeze into the study with a pot of coffee and a plate of *langues de chats*, pat me lightly on the shoulder, breeze out again and the next thing I find is a note on the kitchen table saying you've gone. What is this 'spiritual growth'? Don't they sell it at Dingles? That was a joke. I never make jokes so this must be serious.

Why, Domina? Why not leave me, as in capital D; separate bank accounts, I'll have the TV, you have the deep freeze? I don't know whether you stopped to think about it, but what am I supposed to tell people who come round asking for you? 'Oh no, buddy, she hasn't left me exactly, just gone in search of "herself". What's that? How long will she *be*?' Minnie sweetest, how long does it take? How long will you need? I mean, are we talking in terms of a month or a cosmic year? Like you say, I'm the eternal adolescent, so I can't really conceive what timescale you're functioning on.

I miss you. I just tried to open a can of beans and I cut my finger and I don't know where the elastoplasts are so I'm dripping gore into a box of Kleenex. The latter are 'Mansize'; could this be the long-awaited commercial recognition of the male right to cry through *Whistle Down the Wind* fourth time around? OK, OK, so it doesn't wash – I can open cans, and you know I never cry into anything but crisp, white linen ironed by you, but I *do* miss you.

Have I forgotten something? I remembered your birthday. I reminded *you* about La Mamma Isobella's. We don't have an anniversary (surely *that* isn't the problem?). I know I'm never God's gift to womankind when I'm writing, but then your concentration isn't perfect when you're bringing forth.

I miss you. *Now.*

If you wanted a little break, you could have said the magic word and I'd have taken you on a romantic weekend to Bath. If you'd wanted a holiday we could have taken that trip across North Africa we've been promising ourselves ever since we sat through that dreadful movie about ... what was it called? ... anyway, the one about Moroccan flesh-pots. That's not a bad idea. Just give me another week or two. You can decide how we get there and book the tickets, and we can go. At long last we can go to North Africa and drift in a barge down the Nile, and be cruel about Rick's friend Larry Durrell. No?

Fine. Swell. I *understand, Mina.* Just give me a month and I'll give you a month. I am going to play that elusive creature, the sympathetic male. I won't fuss, I won't go to pieces, I'll keep you informed and I'll leave the emotional blackmail to the abominable Bingham. And if you don't come home in a month, I'll pay you the ultimate compliment of dropping everything and coming to find you. I trust this will be appreciated.

Big, strong, understanding love

from

Randy.

PS Can you remember what to do when the washing machine goes 'fluggudder-fluggudder' instead of 'chugga-chugga-chug'?

7

'Domina Tey!'

Domina turned on the porch steps, her hands full of shopping, her head full of the letter she had read in the taxi. A coach was disgorging its load onto the pavement and she stared blankly across the crowd. She felt deflated and in need of a bath. She hoped she had misheard.

'Domina. Over here, you goose!'

She looked the other way and saw him. Oh my God. Gerald Mannisty.

'Gerald. My God. It's been ages.' He still looked like Rupert Brooke, only a corrupted version that had lived rather more and longer. 'Gerald, you look wonderful.'

Jumping the steps, he swept her into a characteristic hug.

'Cow. You make me look ancient. You've had your hair done – I can smell it – and you've bought lots of clothes.' He cast an expert eye over the names on her bags. 'And you're about to go into the seediest building in Inverness Terrace and I want to know why. You're meant to be in that vast house in Clifton, paying the bills while Randy writes another turgid critique. Don't tell me ... You haven't ... ?' Gerald rounded baby blue eyes in expectation. Domina fumbled in her handbag for her keys.

'We can't talk out here,' she said. 'Come upstairs and all will be revealed.'

'You are a brute! Why did I have to meet you? I was spending a happy, slummy afternoon . . .'

'Yes, what *are* you doing round here?'

'Sauna, darling. There's a rather good one just across the road. The Hermes. Haven't you seen the neon flashing at nights?'

'I haven't spent a night here yet. I only arrived this morning.'

'*How* exciting! I want to come up and sit on the end of your bath, drinking your gin and having a damned good bitch, but it's someone's birthday and I've got to drop off a prezzy. Can we eat?'

'Come back as soon as you've done with whoever it is. Who is it?'

'Horrid girl, really. Fenella Foy. Know her? Very, *very* rich, but got a mouth like a rat-trap, so probably mean as hell to boot. I'll be back around eight-thirty.'

'Wonderful.'

He took her face in his long, firm hands and planted a kiss on her brow.

'God, what fun. Taxi! 'Bye, darling.'

''Bye.'

As Domina turned the key, she noticed that her name had been added to the line-up by the door-bells: 'Mrs Tey – ring twice.' Above her piece of card, and by the same bell, was another: 'Quintus Harding – ring once.' She let herself in and walked down to the kitchen to unload the food she had bought.

The kitchen was the largest basement room. It had an old gas stove, a walk-in larder, a broad deal table that could have been of the same vintage as the house, and an assortment of chairs. Standing at the sinks, one could look through the high windows on to the area at the front and up to an assortment of passing ankles.

As she came down, Domina stood aside to make way for the Asian who had passed her her typewriter in the morning. He was clutching a large cardboard box to his chest, resting his chin on the lid.

'No, no, I insist,' he said, and also stood aside. Domina despised the dances that could ensue on these occasions, so she accepted and carried on her way.

'Thanks,' she said.

At the table sat an old trout in tweeds and thick glasses, whom she assumed to be Avril, and a wafer-thin young man in a white T-shirt and tight jeans.

'Hello,' she said, on her way to her shelf.

'Hello,' said Avril, 'you must be Mrs Tey. Tilly's just told us all about you. My name's Avril, Avril Gilchrist, and this is Thierry Kalbach. Very little English,' she added, with no approach to an undertone.

Domina turned with her sweetest smile. 'How d'you do,' she said to Avril, and to Thierry, '*Bonsoir.*'

'*Ah, vous n'êtes pas française, Madame?*' he asked quickly.

'*Non, mais je le parle un peu.*'

Thierry rose from the table like a Quaker inspired and engaged Domina in conversation as she unloaded the food and walked up to the hall again. Her French was rusty but this did not seem to be important. He had a sweet, well-scrubbed face.

'That terrible old bat,' he went on, 'she has to talk to somebody and knows that as I have little English, I am, how you say in your language, "easy lay", and so she traps me and will not let me go. But I have found that she has no

French, so, if I can speak French, it shuts her up and I can escape. *Je m'excuse*, I should have shaken hands. How d'you do?' They stopped on the landing and he shook hands with a studied air.

'What do you do?' she asked.

'I'm a waiter. At the moment I work in Holland Park Avenue, but I don't think I stay there much longer. Terrible tips and the food . . . *épouvantable*! How about you?'

'Oh. I was a teacher, but I'm between jobs at the moment. Just looking. You know.'

'I know.' They had evidently reached Thierry's door.

'So nice to have met you,' he faltered, in English.

'Not at all,' she grinned. 'It was a pleasure to save you.'

'We strike a bargain. You save me from her each day, and I improve your French.' They laughed and Domina carried on to her room.

She kicked off her shoes, peeled off her tights then, sitting on the edge of her bed, opened bag after bag. She spread out the booty on the counterpane, pulling off pins and price tags as she did so. It included a full skirt in a rough cotton with bold uneven stripes down it in brickish red and a smoky blue. She could wear that, the new white blouse and her old blue pumps. The latter showed off her ankles so well, and she recalled that Gerald had always taken a passionate interest in her ankles. She turned on her radio and found a programme of 'Golden Oldies'. She tossed off her clothes and pulled on her dressing gown. Minutes later, with a towel over her shoulders, stiff pink gin in one hand and the radio and bottle of overpriced bubble bath in the other, she wound her way, barefoot, to an empty bathroom and locked herself in.

8

Domina downed two aspirin and a mug of strong, black coffee. Then she bought a *Times* and fled to a bench by the Round Pond to collect her thoughts.

Gerald had left at some ungodly hour, she had been half asleep and could remember only the pleasure of being left with the whole of a single bed. Dinner had been a good idea, just what she had needed. He had steered her to his favourite 'dive' of the moment, an as yet undiscovered Vietnamese restaurant in a Pimlico basement. As they had settled into their corner table and giggled at the Piaf coming over the speaker system, it had dawned on them that they had not once eaten alone since Gerald's last year at Cambridge.

Gerald had been two years above Domina. Nocturnal event number five, he had suffused her first university summer with a daft, pink glow. Theirs had been the first proper affair of her life. Neither of them had taken the thing seriously, which on reflection explained how they managed to spin it out for so long. Gerald was the outstanding economist of his year, yet had set his heart on becoming an actor. He won a place at RADA, then gave up after a year of the course. He had written to Domina announcing this move, the only expression of genuine disenchantment she had known him to make. He realized, he wrote, that university drama was, like university politics or journalism, a cipher. He had acted because it was the most efficacious way of making people take notice in an atmosphere of fierce social competition. He was doing quite well at RADA, he wrote, but he was no fool. There was little point in trying to become an actor unless one had the makings of a great one, which he did not. He did, however, have the makings of a vast fortune in the shape of a bevy of rich prats from King's who were begging him to invest their inheritances for them. The Stock Exchange was unaesthetic, certainly, he went on, but just think of the bliss unparalleled of an early retirement. Domina could be arty, he would make a mint, and then he would take her to Glyndebourne every year to quiet his conscience. In the event, he had taken her to Glyndebourne only once, and that was with Polly Schreiber, the other half of a disastrous marriage that was now in the last stages of its dissolution.

Dinner had been just what she needed. Volley after ego-buffing volley of social venom. Then, by the time they were ordering tinned lychees for a laugh, and had dissected the failures of their several friends, the wine took effect, the conversation turned in on themselves, and Domina had found herself telling Gerald, through a fog of tears, that she had run away to London because she could not face middle-age. Then Gerald, who as always was not quite as drunk as his companion, turned on his highly-sexed uncle routine and said he wanted them to go back for cocoa at her place and prove that the vitality of their suspended passion was undimmed. Then she had said yes please, and found herself letting him in at the front door of Inverness Terrace. He had read the card marked: 'Mrs Tey – ring twice' in a voice that seemed hideously funny at the time, and they had giggled all the way to the attic.

Installed in her room, Gerald had given her Gordon's instead of cocoa, and had proceeded to remove her clothes. The gin had sent her into new realms of hilarity and she had danced a tango with him. At each swing of the dance, he had removed an article of his clothing, and by the time she heard the knock at the door, he had begun to get very excited indeed. Had Domina been a fraction more in control, she would have put her finger to her lips and waited for the knocking to go away; as it was, she clutched her new skirt to her chest and stuck her head around the door.

He was slightly taller than her, which made him about six foot. He had light brown hair which curled at the edges, thin lips and sea-green eyes. He looked anorexic. Seeing him dithering there in dressing gown, winceyette pyjamas and corduroy slippers, she could barely control the impulse to drop her skirt and fling wide the door. The innocence of his glance was sobering, however, so she smiled gaily and asked,

'Yes?'

'Oh. Sorry to disturb you, but –' A young voice. Twenty or twenty-one, she surmised. His eyes remained firmly on her face. She wished her nipples could whistle to attract his attention. 'I wonder if you could possibly be a little quieter,' he ventured. 'You see it is quite late.'

'Is it?' She really had no idea.

'Yes, and actually, we're not supposed to have guests after midnight.'

'Sorry,' she whispered. His prudery was insufferable. 'I'll try not to do it again.' And she shut the door in his face, very gently.

*

'Ciggie. Here, Ciggie! Come on, Cigarette.' A young girl called her cocker spaniel, waving a stick as she did so. 'Go on, Ciggie!' She hurled it into the water and the dog obediently leapt in, struggled bravely through the little waves, and retrieved the thing for her. 'Good girl. Good, *good* Cigarette.' She stroked the head lovingly, then tossed the stick back into the water. 'Go on, Ciggie. Go on. Fetch!'

Domina watched as the spaniel plunged back in, sending the ducks churning to either side.

Looking back, it would have been better to have thrown Gerald out at that juncture, but then, without underwear one is somehow of diminished moral stature. What followed was quite unexpected and deeply disturbing. She had remembered him as a gentle lover, courteous, solicitous even. Fifteen years of the Stock Exchange and Polly Schreiber had left their mark. Now he was rough. He didn't just nibble – she liked that – he spanked her. He slapped her face. He even spat. What shocked Domina most was that, while a part of her sat soberly up and said this is sordid and unnatural, the other drunken, active part of her lay back and enjoyed it. She let the overweight War Poet spit in her face. As she stared balefully at the reiterated errands of the swimming dog, she recoiled from the recollection that she had gone so far as to participate in his verbal fantasies. 'You're the Boss,' she had moaned, 'no one's allowed to do this but you 'cause you're the Boss.'

He had fallen asleep immediately it was over. She had lain on the outside of that hopelessly single bed, one foot resting on the carpet, and heard music. It had been very soft and it had come from that boy's room. Quintus Harding. A piece of Gregorian chant, it had taken her back to spring mornings in the convent gardens. *Cum veni Sancti Spiritu*. She had passed out while trying to remember the translation, and failing to summon more than 'Come Holy Ghost our souls inspire, and lighten with celestial fire.'

Domina shuddered and tried to read her paper. The sun was now almost overhead and she could feel it on her skin. Her fingers were still puffed from the long, therapeutic soak she had taken on waking. The painkillers were keeping the headache at bay; there was only a vague throb – more a distortion of sounds than a pain. The children of Bayswater were throwing stale bread to the geese and ducks. A herring gull and a bevy of bustling pigeons were muscling in on the treat. Behind her a man's voice, Californian, and a little girl on the brink of tantrum:

'We're going home to Mummy.'

'Nooo!'

'Please, *Señora*?' A Spanish girl, about fifteen, stood at her shoulder behind the bench. She held out a camera. Behind her a group of five or six other girls were crouching, tittering on the grass. 'Please. You take our picture. Yes?'

'OK.' Domina accepted the camera, a small, stylized one with minimal controls. She aimed it at the Spaniards. 'Smile,' she commanded. They obeyed. All overweight, they smiled and laughed. Domina fired.

'Thank you so much.' The ringleader took back her machine. 'Goodbye.'

Domina stood. The breeze that had been so cooling across the water had dropped. It was becoming an extremely hot day. She folded the newspaper and set off towards the Serpentine. She reached *Physical Energy*, Watt's horse and rider that seemed about to gallop up through the air over Kensington Palace. Her father had made her admire it as a child, but she had never ceased to find it indecent. The offence had something to do with the man's muscle-bound feet. It was sexy, though, beyond question; the grip of his thick, naked thighs on the animal's flanks was spectacular. As she walked past, she noticed that someone had marked the podium with the red-painted plea: 'Free Nelson Mandela' and that this in turn had been half daubed out by a National Front symbol in white. The piece certainly had fascist overtones.

Hitler's Olympics. The nearest she had come to a row with Randy in recent years had been over those. She had championed Leni Riefenstahl's *Olympia* as an example of documentary rising above propaganda, he had made a scene, and they had been forced to leave the dinner party in an unseemly rush.

Domina stopped at the crest of the slope. On one side the path ran back to the Bayswater Road, on the other to the avenue and so to the Albert Memorial. Before her lay the Serpentine. She had a sudden hankering to see Peter Pan and set out to do so. It was only when she was half-way through the trees to her right that she flushed with irritation at the failure of her memory. She knew the Orangery, and Pram Walk, and the Memorial, and that fountain with the little dog in it, but she could not remember how to find Peter Pan. She kept walking, just the same, in the hope that she would find a map, then her foot caught on something and she fell. She was quite unhurt, and the ground was dry. She had even managed to fall unseen.

It was a goose. A long-necked Canada goose, and it was dead. She jumped into a crouching position with a little cry and reached out a hand. Beneath the feathers the flesh was still slightly warm. She knew nothing whatever about birds, but assumed that there must be a heart. She moved a palm rapidly about its chest, feeling for a flicker of life. There was nothing. Gingerly she reached a hand beneath it and turned it over. There was no blood, no apparent damage. The plumage was quite unharmed.

The sound of distant children made up Domina's mind. She had to get the poor thing out of sight. It was outrageous that a keeper should not have found out already and buried it. Anyone might see it. She stood and brushed the leaves off her skirt, then she laid her *Times* open on the grass and rolled the goose into it. Using the paper as an improvised cradle (there were no worms or blood, but she was wary lest something seep out) she held the corpse in her arms and set off the way she had come. She left the path at the slope, knowing there was a keeper's outhouse down in the shrubberies where people fed the squirrels. The neck proved a problem. It kept swinging awkwardly against her thighs. She tried to hold its beak in the fingers of one hand but it proved too slippery and left her grasp almost at once. No children were in sight, which was a blessing. It didn't really matter if there was no one in the outhouse to deal with the bird, so long as she could get it well out of the way.

Suddenly she was aware of a dog's bark approaching her from behind. She turned quickly, sending the goose's head flailing at her waist, to see a large dog, like an Alsatian, only black. It was bounding down the hill, no owner in sight, and it appeared to be slavering.

'No,' cried Domina vaguely, and it was upon her. The dog wasted no time in seizing the goose by the neck that swung so temptingly within his reach. He seized and pulled surprisingly hard, in short fierce jerks. Because of the newspaper, Domina's hold on the dead bird was far from firm. She could feel the body slipping at every tug. 'No. No! Let go, you filthy animal! *Bad!*' she shouted. Still he tugged, growling savagely on each effort and staring up at her with undisguised loathing for trying to stop his fun. Someone appeared on the crest of the hill. They were carrying a lead. The dog tugged again and this time the corpse almost left Domina's grasp. She lost her temper and lashed out with a foot at his mouth. This only made the matter worse, for she all but lost her balance and he became enraged, shaking his head from side to side. Then the figure on the hill shouted.

'No. Please don't kick him. Japhet, get down! Japh! Here, boy!' The youth ran down the hill and let out a piercing whistle with both fingers in his mouth. At once the dog relinquished his prey and ran back to his master with a welcoming bark or two.

Domina was near to tears. She wrapped the goose more firmly in its *Times* and prepared a harangue.

'You ought to keep him more under control, you know . . .' she began, then saw who it was, and stalled.

'Hello. I am sorry. He's still very young and he runs like the wind the moment he's off the lead,' said Quintus Harding.

'I know. I'm sorry. I shouldn't have shouted. It's just that I found this dead goose and I was trying to take it to the keepers before a child found it . . . or a dog.'

'Goodness. The poor thing. Down, boy.' He made Japhet lie down and came to touch her goose. 'It can't have been dead long.'

'I know. It was still warm when I found it. There's a keeper just down here, I think.' She started to walk on down the hill and found Quintus Harding walking beside her. Japhet was now perfectly docile, and back on a leash.

'I'm sorry about last night,' Quintus said suddenly.

'What? Oh that.' Domina flushed. 'I'm sorry I kept you awake.' She felt inordinately coy. 'Old college friend,' she heard herself mutter heartily, 'turned up out of the blue. Hadn't seen each other in ages.'

'It doesn't matter actually.'

'What?'

'The rule about guests after midnight. That's probably why Tilly didn't tell you. She only has it to stop people sharing a room for one person's rent. She doesn't care about the general comings and goings. Thierry and Penny have overnight guests all the time.'

'Really?' She noticed that he spoke without a hint of archness or irony. His innocence bordered on the stolid. 'He's a lovely dog. What's his name?'

'Japhet. Normally just Japh; Japhet when you're cross.'

'How does he get on with Tilly's dachshund . . . Beverly?'

'You mean Grace.'

'Yes. Grace.'

'They've never met. Japhet isn't mine. He's Brother Jerome's. I just take him for walks.'

'Brother Jerome?'

'He's my tutor at the Greek Orthodox chaplaincy off Moscow Road.'

'Ah. I see,' said Domina, and tucked the goose's head into her hand again.

9

Royal York Crescent

Bristol 8

Avon

Darling Mina,

Randy's just told me that you've gone to visit your sick mother, which can mean only one thing. I'll type the envelope for this and post it from the city centre in the hope that he won't know who it's from and will forward it to wherever you're hiding.

Christ, Domina, you little fool! Why didn't you feel you could tell me if something was wrong? I could see you were getting pissed off with his endless hours in that poky little study, but I had no idea there was anything worse. There is something worse, isn't there?

My first reaction was Oh my God, it's something I said, but then I got home and Rick told me not to be so self-centred. He said that of course nothing I said could make you leave Randy, it would just stop you talking to me for a bit. But then I thought really hard about the things I've been telling you recently and that worried me. I know you all think I'm just a dreary old lush who's foul to everyone, then can't remember a thing the next morning, but I *do* remember, Mina, honestly I do.

I remember laying into Rick night after night. I can remember everything I said to Randy at that disastrous New Year's Eve party last year. More to the point, I remember all I've ever said to you while in my cups.

I make no bones about the fact that I'm jealous of you. I've always been jealous of you ever since I had to do props for *The Rose and the Ring* at school. One could say it has given my life its sense of purpose. I've always been jealous and you've always known it. Neither of us can do a thing about the jealousy – it's just there, the fact that you have always had the things that I've always wanted – but *I* should have been able to do something about the spiteful things it makes me say. I haven't, and I'm sorry.

Mina, I'm rambling and you know why. Whether or not your running away in this ridiculous fashion is anything to do with me, I *feel guilty*. There. I've said my bit and now I feel much better and can face dinner at the Croxley-Hills'. I shall think of you, as I start slagging off that bitch's lifestyle, somewhere between the second glass of calvados and the front door.

And if there's 'someone else', I am hurt that I haven't been told and I demand to know who they are at once.

Love as ever, etc. etc.

Ginny B.

PS At the theatre board meeting this morning I threatened a Harold Heartburne for the autumn and was almost strung up by the heels.

Apparently from Fi Templeton down to the lowliest ASM they want to do a revival of *Sinful Living*, so that is exactly what we'll do.

Isn't that sweet?

10

'Fantastic, Domina,' said the girl in the secretarial agency. 'If you can give us a buzz around half-past five, we'll let you know if we've found you any work for tomorrow.'

Something in these words took a profound hold on Domina and, as she walked back along Notting Hill Gate, she was transfixed by a pang of homesickness. The next eight hours were spent in a sustained and vain combat with the forces of cowardly regret. She bought herself a bag of nectarines and ate them on the top of the eighty-eight bus which she rode to the back door of the Tate, where she passed a valiant hour and a half wandering from room to airy room. The Tate was a favourite gallery; as a rule, the Early English collection never failed to lighten her heart. Today the women looked cold and fat, their lovers insipidly complacent. She drifted into the bookshop to stock up on postcards and spoilt herself with a new study of Fuseli's life and works. Still the ache persisted. Mindful of the axiom that the gloom of friends is the best cure for one's own, she telephoned Des and invited her out to tea.

Fortnum's felt dowdy and airless. Des was late, as ever, so Domina went upstairs ahead of her and ordered herself Earl Grey and cinnamon toast. A Senior Wives Fellowship coach party, up for the day, were spread around several tables nearby. From the flashing of catalogues and paper bags, she gathered that they came fresh from the Royal

Academy. She amused herself by eavesdropping, and the toast had the perfect balance of sweet crunch and warming spice, so by the time Des waddled into view, her clouds were already lifting.

'Hello, Des darling.'

'Hello you,' snapped Des, blowing her nose.

'Not hay fever?'

'No, a bloody awful cold, and yes, isn't it odd having one at this time of year?'

'Poor thing,' tinkled Domina. 'Have some of my tea and toast while I order some more.' She couldn't help noticing Des wince with pain as she sat down. The woman's hand flew protectively to her armpit. 'Are you OK, Des?'

'Fine. Honestly. Just a touch of cramp,' said Des, and fumbled for her Woodbines while her client poured her some tea. Domina supposed that she was suffering in silence. If illness were in the offing she would worm out the truth. 'How's the Great Adventure?' Des asked.

'Great. Oh yes, could we have another pot of . . . you prefer Darjeeling, don't you Des? . . . yes, a pot of Darjeeling please,' Domina told the elderly waitress who was hovering, 'and another round of cinnamon toast would be lovely. Thanks.'

'She's come back,' Des intoned, as soon as the coast was clear.

'Sorry. Who?'

'Stella. Arnold's wife.'

Mustering a suitably pained expression, Domina ransacked her memory and found one Arnold, a biochemistry teacher who had moved in with Des when his wife walked out on him a year ago. She had only met him once, at an outlandish North London bonfire party at the Peakes'. He had sported a beard and open-toed sandals.

'Oh God. Des, what'll happen?'

'He'll go back to her, I suppose, now that there's no need to cry on my shoulder.'

'When did she come back?'

'He rang up last night. Said he'd got back from work and found her suitcase in his bedroom and her smalls drying over the bath. Said he thought he should stay over there for the night to see what was going on.'

'But does he still love . . . ?'

'I never knew he could sound so animated,' she went on bitterly, exhaling smoke between her teeth and crushing the stub in welcome to the new round of toast. 'Getting ready to wheel her out the fatted calf.'

'Will she stay?'

'I expect so. For a year or two. It was her third runner, you know. I was his third Mother Earth. D'you want that other piece of toast?'

'All yours.'

'Thanks.' Des took the last piece of cinnamon toast and munched on it, lugubrious. 'Go on, then. Tell me your news,' she said.

'Oh. Well. Nothing much,' sighed Domina, feeling quite recovered and trying not to show it. 'I applied for what Ginny Bingham would call "real work" this morning.'

'I thought you'd come here to write.'

'And recharge my batteries. If I were going to sit in my room all day, I might as well have stayed in Clifton.'

'What kind of work? You're not qualified to do anything.'

'I can type, though. I registered at Westminster Bureau to be a temp. It's bloody good pay, you know. I'd always thought of typists as the City's little skivvies, but they must be rolling. Three-ninety an hour.'

'Doctor Turner?' The elderly waitress was hovering once more.

'Yes?' asked Des.

'There's a telephone call for you. A lady called Imogen Kramer.'

'Thanks. Here I come.'

'*Very* impressive,' said Domina. 'Who is she?'

'Just another abortive little scheme of mine.' Des stood and followed the waitress to the telephone. Domina went to wash the stickiness off her hands and to dab on some scent. When she returned to the table, Des was still away. She looked in her bag for some other diversion. The girl at the agency had given her a green plastic satchel. It said 'Westminster Bureau – Total Temping Package' on the outside. She pulled it out to take a proper look: Pen, pencil, rubber, shorthand notebook, pocket spelling dictionary and a button-mending kit. Very neat; nothing missing but a packet of tampons.

Des was almost skipping across the carpet. She was radiant. Something was badly wrong.

'I don't believe it,' she laughed, 'I simply don't believe it!' This time, as she sat down, she actually cried out.

'Des, are you ill?'

'No, no,' Des snapped, almost angrily, 'I said – it's just cramp. But listen. Amazing news!'

'What is it? Who is this Kramer woman?'

'She's going to buy V.J. Muldoon!'

'Never!'

'You should know her, she works on the new women's venture at Pharos.'

'You know they never tell me anything.'

'Well, she wrote to me a few weeks back,' Des was gabbling with excitement, she snatched a tremulous pause to light up a Woodbine, 'wrote to me and bowled me over by saying she'd been trying to trace Old Muldoon's trustees because she was convinced she was due for a revival. Dished me up a load of crap about how *Jessamine* carried a vital message for the Women's Movement.'

'And?' If Domina had brightened her smile any further, her face would have split.

'That was her now. She's talked to the board and they're prepared to make an absurdly inflated offer for the whole lot. She even wants to produce a boxed set.'

Des had been left sole trustee of the novels of her great-grandmother, who had written under the alias 'V.J. Muldoon', had scarcely been *le dernier cri* in her own day, and had been long out of print by her great-granddaughter's. Des and Domina had come to use 'Muldoon' as a private word for obscure penury. In Domina's mind, that Des was marked out to be the guardian of these understandably neglected works had set the seal on the comfortable fact of her financial dependence. Now she had to sit, croaking happy platitudes, and hear of the fresh career awaiting *Jessamine*, *Gardyner's Folly* and their kin.

To expiate her envious indignation, she gave Des the new Fuseli book with a convincing spontaneous sparkle before she fell into a taxi. This meant that she now had nothing to read in bed, so she stopped at Hornton Street to enrol in the public library. She walked home over Campden Hill clutching some of the novels she had been meaning to read ever since they won prizes three or more years ago. She lay in a sweaty heap in the armchair in her room, rejecting each in turn, switching off the evening's Prom, writing and throwing away letters to Randy and the Hateful Bingham. With no television to fill the void of the night ahead, she forced herself to wait until eight o'clock before racing downstairs to cook herself something with the curiosities she had brought home from a health shop. The consequent tofu chowder was disgusting, but she was obliged to eat the lot by the hope that someone would come down to share the vast, empty table with her. No one did. The house remained unexpectedly silent. She washed up her plate and saucepan and climbed the stairs to the attic where, with the aid of a toothmugful of gin and water (Gerald had managed to shatter the Angosturas bottle) she had a damned good cry and sobbed her way into an early night.

11

It was twelve-fifty a.m. and Domina needed a bowl of muesli. The cry had left her eyelids sore, but it had released the tension. As she walked stiffly to her fridge and took out the milk, she recalled having cried 'Voglio mia Mamma', through her tears, which was a bad sign and increased the necessity of a midnight feast.

'Blast!' The cereal was still on her shelf in the larder. She pulled her dressing gown around her, dropped her keys into the pocket, and set out for the kitchen with her milk.

The house was now alive. Radios chuckled from behind closed doors, and people were taking baths. Mr Punjabi was using the telephone on the stairs; at least, he was hold-ing the receiver to one ear. He grinned and said, 'Good evening, Mrs Tey,' as she passed him. Domina turned off the chilly tiles in the hall onto the basement staircase, and heard voices from the kitchen. Hearing a girl's tones as well as Thierry's, she ran her fingers through her hair before pushing open the door.

Thierry was standing at the stove, making crêpes and giggling. A girl, with abundant peroxide hair, was apply-ing make-up and finishing a can of Diet Coke. At the other end of the table sat a boy, eighteen or nineteen, who toyed shyly with a glass of wine. As Domina entered, all three heads turned and the giggling stopped.

'Hi,' she enthused, feeling she had stepped on a Red Admiral. Thierry span round, pan in hand.

'Domina, how absolutely lovely it is to see you!' he declared in faultless Onslow Square. 'May I introduce Miss Penelope Havers?'

'Hi.'

'. . . And Mr Billy . . . er . . . Billy.'

'Hello.'

'Hello, I'm Domina. I moved into the attic on Tuesday,' said Domina, finding her muesli and a bowl and joining them at the table. 'Just thought I'd have a midnight snack,' she added, by way of explanation. Billy stared deeper into his glass and the girl was rapt in smearing a perfect scarlet sheen across her lips. Domina escaped into French. 'How was work this evening, Thierry?'

'I can't stand it much longer. I think I must hand in my notice. As you see, the food is so horrible I have to cook my own! I think I'll get a friend to swop. We do that, you see; we get bored, so we swop jobs from time to time. I think I'll go to Blanchflore's – the food there, *c'est exquis.* You want a crêpe? I've made far too many.'

'No thanks. I'm sure the three of you . . .'

'I've eaten,' said Penny. She rose, tossing her hair back off her face. Her body unfurled from beneath the table. Her heels were inordinately long, and red. 'Mustn't be late for work,' she muttered. 'Terry, I'll see you 'round, OK? Nice to have met you, Mrs Tey. 'Bye, er, Billy.'

Everyone said goodbye and she was gone. Thierry slung down two plates of steaming crêpes and a bowl of sugar. He felt in his jacket pocket and produced a miniature bottle of orange fluid which he tipped over his creations.

'Grand Marnier,' he explained to Billy. 'I filch it from behind the bar.'

Domina found she had been waiting for them to begin before she ate. She took a mouthful. It was good, full of pieces of nut and dried apricot and fig. She felt stronger.

'What does she do? I thought she was an actress.'

'Actress?' Thierry started incredulously. 'Well, only for audiences of one at a time. *C'est time fille de joie, Madame.*'

'Oh,' said Domina, unsure whether to sound surprised. She sought to involve Thierry's guest. 'Do you work in the same restaurant, Billy?'

Startled, he looked up and blushed. 'No ... I ...' he began.

'*Non. Non. Je l'ai trouvé en revenant. C'est un ange, qui ne parle pas français.*'

Billy looked from one to the other without understanding and smiled at last, a fresh, white smile which disarmed and justified. He seemed quite happy to sit and listen, so Domina chatted to his host awhile, asking him about his family.

Thierry hailed from Saint Malo. His father was an insurance clerk. His mother was fat and pious, it seemed, but worthy of respect on account of her mystic understanding with pastry. He had a brother called Yannick who was married and studying to be an architect, and a little sister called Véronique who was still at the stage of wanting to be a nun.

There were footsteps on the stairs and Avril opened the door. In a flash the crêpe plates were in the sink and it had been perceived that *pauvre Guillaume* was exhausted and must be taken to bed immediately. The muesli had now quite woken Domina. If she went to bed she would only lie and brood. She stayed to feed the insatiable appetite for character.

'Hello there. Dormy feasts?' asked Avril.

'Yes. Isn't it fun? Just like being back at school. Would you like a bowlful?'

'No, thanks awfully. It catches on my plate.' Avril slumped into a chair and tapped the ash of her cigarette into the Diet Coke can. She was still in tweeds and stout brown shoes.

'Have you just got in?' asked Domina, placing her age at about fifty-four.

'No. On my way out, actually. Off to work.'

Not wishing to jump to alarming conclusions, Domina trod her way with care. 'Tilly told me you were a writer.' She delivered the statement as a question.

'Yes. I'm off to do some research. All very thrilling. Rent boys in Piccadilly. I'm far too early, I know, but I can't afford to take taxis everywhere, so I've got to grab the last tube then hang around Leicester Square with my thermos till I can find "a piece of the action", as they say.'

'Rent boys?'

'Boy prostitutes. There are hundreds of them, you know. It's like the eighteen-eighties all over again. They come from the provinces – especially the Midlands and the North – hoping pathetically to find work, and end up on the streets. People assume that happens to girls, but for the most part it's their younger brothers.'

'Really?'

'Oh yes. You see, dear, girls are more circumspect. Most

girls who turn up down here have gained some skill in advance. Typing, for instance. Women aren't as romantic as men.'

'I went to one of those typing agencies today.'

'My dear, I thought you were a teacher,' said Avril with a look of deep concern.

'I am. But I won't find a teaching post just like that. It's usually a matter of having interviews for posts that won't be vacant for months ahead. But I can type, so I thought I could join the monstrous regiment of temps while I waited.'

'What a stroke of luck. You don't ever consider doing transcript work?'

'I love it. I learnt to type to help my husband with his sermons, in fact.'

Avril was excited. She had lit another Camel. When she exhaled she waved her cigarette hand like a fan before her face to disperse the smoke. Her grey-blue coiffure was a ragged, once-every-two-months job. This emphasized the loose, canine quality of her face. Her nose was long as a setter's and her mouth dropped on either side so that the lower lip kept being pulled up into place to hold back the dribble. There was a marked droop to one of the eyes as well; perhaps there had been a stroke.

'Now tell me what you charge.'

'Oh Lord. I haven't the faintest . . .'

'Because the only girl I've managed to find quoted me something absurd.'

'Well, why don't you quote me something less?'

'Right you are. Seventy-five pence a page, and I supply paper and carbons and so forth.'

'Fine. I can start tomorrow. I've got a machine in my room.'

'Well, there is one thing I'd have to sort out.'

'Yes?' said Domina with a helpful smile.

'I know this sounds odd, but I really must be able to rely on your discretion. It's a very delicate matter. I'm using false names throughout, of course, but I'm only getting half my material by swearing absolute secrecy. If they were to find out that a third party was involved things could take a rather nasty turn.'

Domina kept a straight face. Just.

'Is it a novel?' she enquired.

'Heavens, no. I'm not nearly imaginative enough. No, I'm what's called a ghost writer.'

'Oh, I see: autobiography. Do I know them?'

'Not unless you're a regular visitor to Wandsworth Jail.'

'Ah,' said Domina, trying to react as befitted a late canon's spouse.

'Yes. All very thrilling, as I say, but rather tricky. I was put in touch with him by a friend who does visiting. No one she knows personally, you understand. She goes to chat to the ones who don't have any family, or any family who'll recognize them, that is. She sent me along, said I'd find something to my advantage, and there's this poor chap aching to tell his life story.'

'Why . . . er?'

'Matricide, among other things. Worked his way up through petty crime, ran away to London and became a successful rent boy and then drugs peddler. Then he started getting visitations – very strict Methodist upbringing working on the LSD if you ask me – and some holy voice told him to kill his mother.'

'Goodness!'

'Yes. Rather a loose woman, I understand. Anyway, they didn't believe the story of the voices. The verdict was that he was guilty of murder etc. etc., and that the religious element was a cunning invention to try to swing the jury. The mad ones often get better treatment, apparently.'

'And now?'

'Oh, he still gets the visions. Visions, voices, promptings from within, or above or below – hard to tell, actually. The biggest trouble is that he is totally illiterate and not especially articulate to boot. He has *no* written evidence for me to go on, and the family refuses to co-operate. I have only his fairly incoherent ramblings to go by and they're thin at their best.'

'So you have to make things up?'

'Not exactly. But most of us ghosters have to feel where the characters need a little plumping out. Where an episode is important to the storyline and you only have the bare bones, you obviously have to improvise a bit of dialogue, too.'

'What fun!'

'Yes. But tricky fun as I say, because even with false names, you don't want to go misrepresenting things, just in case someone reads the thing who decides to raise merry hell. I won't get a mention on the cover, of course, but these boys can find out anything if they put their minds to it.'

'Well, I can start as soon as you like.'

'Lovely. I'll put what there is under your door. You're on the top, aren't you? By young Quintus?'

'That's right.'

'I must dash or I'll miss the last tube. Many thanks. See you soon.' She swept out by the area steps, jabbing a half-smoked Camel into the Diet Coke can where it sizzled briefly.

Domina felt a yawn coming and welcomed it with a loving stretch. The typing would be amusing. Avril Gilchrist. The name was unfamiliar, but then one never did hear of any 'ghosters'. Picturing the one that had just left, with her Thermos in a plastic string bag, her hounds and horseshoes headscarf and her ugly jewellery, Domina doubted she had met with much success, doubted indeed that she had been published at all. Kensington attracted her sort. Hers was a species that sat taking vigorous notes on park benches, that hounded assistants in the Reference Library, that ended up shuffling sightlessly along Queensway, picking at her filthy clothes and embarrassing shoppers by crying, 'Look at the birdies! Look. Look there, I tell you! They's awatching for the Great Day!'

'Hello, lovie. Couldn't sleep?' Tilly, also in a quilted dressing gown, a cigarette bouncing on her lower lip. She grinned.

'No. I'd been asleep for hours, then I woke up.'

'Always the way. It's the trains underneath; not loud, but they's always there. You'll get used to them in a day or two. I came down to lock up.' She shot the bolt on the street door, then came to sit at the table. Domina stood and washed her bowl before returning. Tilly was peering darkly into the brown paper bag that held the muesli.

'Have some,' suggested Domina, 'it's very good.'

'You must be joking. Hate the stuff. It's all bitty, like guinea-pig food. Can't nick a drop of milk, can I?'

'Go ahead.'

'Nothing I like better at this time of night than a rum nog.' Tilly waddled to the stove with the milk. 'Heat the milk in a saucepan, like so. Don't want it boiling, just swing it around till it's letting off a spot of steam.' Domina listened to the commentary, trying to memorize the speech patterns. 'Then you nicks one of Master Thierry's eggs and beats it up in a mug with a fork, like so. Then,' she produced a half-bottle of dark rum from her pocket with a flourish and a wink, 'you adds a drop of the old brown magic, a pinch of sugar, and last of all . . . you whips in the hot milk.'

'Sounds disgusting.'

'No, honestly. It's great. Here, try a sip.' She sat back in her chair and pushed the brimming mug across the table-top to Domina. Domina hated hot milk, but forced herself to take a sip of the brew, and was surprised to like it.

'You're right. It is good.'

'Told you. You'll never want cocoa again,' Tilly chuckled. 'Met any of the others yet, have you?'

'Yes. I met Quintus in the park today.'

'Oh, he's a duck.'

'Yes. Then this evening I talked to Thierry and Avril and Penny and a boy called Billy.'

'One of Thierry's?'

'I think so.'

'Old Tel's a caution. Different boy every night of the week, just about; never seems to try to keep them. Oh, sorry.'

'What?'

'Well.' Tilly was suddenly covered in embarrassment. 'It

must be the rum, I completely forgot myself for a moment. Oh, Mrs Tey, I'm so sorry. With you being a vicar's widow and that.'

'Oh, for heaven's sake,' Domina laughed, 'I was the vicar's wife, not the vicar himself. And the church is quite "with-it" now, you know. I met young Penny earlier on.'

'Yeah?'

'Yes. She was on her way to work.'

'Oh Gawd.' Tilly laughed now. 'You've been through it all now. I was so afraid you'd want to leave or something – go somewhere more "respectable" like. I'm amazed Quin's stayed as long as he has.'

'I don't see why you worry. Look at Mary Magdalene.'

'Who's she?'

'Oh, just a famous tart.'

'That's it. As soon as they get famous everyone wants to be seen with them. Like that girl what got caught with the MP and the spy.'

'How long has Penny been with you?'

'Over a year, now. It's so sad. She really does want to be an actress.'

'Don't they all say that?'

'Well, I don't know. But she's dead serious. I've seen the photos. She's got lots of photos of things she was in at college and that. Yeah. She went to college and everything. She came up here after her A-levels. She'd got a place at drama school and she lived here and went up there on her bike first thing every morning for about eight months. Dead keen she was. Then her dad got made redundant and she had to give up 'cause he couldn't pay the fees. I said, "Look, love, you can stay here free if that'd be any help." 'Cause I've plenty of rooms, and having one charity guest wouldn't make a bit of difference really. But she's that proud, you know. Wouldn't take a thing. "I'll make it on my own. Somehow, I'll make it on my own," she says. And she does try. She goes to auditions nearly every day. But they always have to say no because she has to have that thing, that liberty card or something.'

'Equity card.'

'That's the one. Anyway, I says to her, "You've got A-levels, now get yourself an office job or something to tide you over while you wait." But she says she can't afford to, in case she had to miss an audition and ruin her chances. So she's on the dole with the rest of them. Apparently, if you've a UB40 to show, you can get free dance classes, so she's learning them all – jazz, tap, classical ballet she can do – the lot.'

'But that's wretched. She must be good to have got into drama school in the first place; the competition's very stiff at those places. Hasn't she any friends there who could help her?'

'No go.'

'She needs some contacts.'

'She's too proud. She'll sell her body before she asks a favour.'

As she mounted the stairs once more, muesli bag under her arm, milk carton in hand, Domina resolved to help the girl. Beneath all the make-up her face had been striking. Ginny had at least one Equity card virtually in her gift each year. She would get her to audition Penny. Bingham could write out of the blue, in her role as director of the Bristol company, saying something about recommendations from the school. Even if she was hopeless, it would boost her ego. Ginny could always make her a walk-on.

Radiating virtue, Domina climbed into bed and fell asleep mentally composing a letter to Randy.

12

It was another morning. It was Thursday morning, the eighth of August. An electric buzzing sounded twice outside her door. Domina lay and stared at some flies describing squares near the ceiling. Something had woken her. She wondered why. The two buzzes came again. She lifted her eyes from the bed and sought out the face of her alarm clock. Half-past ten. She swore and sat up violently. Someone banged on the door.

'Here. There's someone at the front door for you.'

The charwoman. Domina swung her feet to the floor and swung her dressing gown about her shoulders. Mrs Moorhouse was leaning on her hoover on the landing. She stared blankly at Domina's emerging form.

'Here. There's someone at the front door for you,' she said again. 'Pick up the intercom.'

Domina obediently lifted the receiver. There was a click and a woman's voice asked:

'Domina? Domina, *cara*, is that you?' Domina held the receiver away from her ear and looked back at Mrs Moorhouse's stony face.

'It's my mother,' she told her.

'Well, press that button on the box.'

Domina pressed the button on the box, wishing it could make her caller go away. Her heart quickened as she heard the distant clatter of the electric lock in the hall and a pair of feet advancing over the tiles. Ignoring Mrs Moorhouse's stare, she turned back into her room and started to tidy things as best she could. By the time Isobella had exhausted the possibilities of the other floors, she might even have found some clothes. Instinctively, she threw together the semblance of breakfast on a tray. She began to make her bed, then heard Mrs Moorhouse betray her.

'She's up here, room number twelve.'

'Shit,' said Domina and sat heavily on her bed, running her fingers through her hair. There was a clipped knock at the door and it opened.

'Domina?'

'Mamma. What a lovely surprise.' She looked up as Isobella glided in, dropping bags and stretching out her hands in greeting. She had always asked to be called Mamma with her native accent, an affectation that heightened the operatic feel of her arrivals and departures.

'Domina, *cara*, what is the meaning of this? What has he done to you? That horrid, horrid Randolph. I never like him. I just count the days. And now . . .' She planted several kisses on her daughter's hair, then stood back in disgust. Now she'll notice the room, thought Domina. 'But this room! *Diamine*, it's worse than my worst dreams! What can you have been thinking of? Look at you. Half-past ten, and my daughter's still undressed and sitting in a maid's room in a slum. It makes me feel so guilty. No, it makes me feel so *ashamed*. Why didn't you tell me?'

'Mamma, please? Just shut up a moment, yes? *Per piacere?*' Domina raised her face to the storm and silenced it. She sat, patting the bed beside her. 'Come,' she said.

Isobella settled beside her. Domina took her hand and

stared deep into her face, a technique she had discovered in her teens for holding her mother's attention. Only Isobella Feraldi would wear such an exquisite hat on a mission to save her daughter from perdition, she reflected. Jealous tongues hinted at surgery, but Domina knew this face to be the real thing; the years had been kind to the point of extravagance. Mamma mixed her scent herself, from little phials she bought from the nuns at home. The smell evoked years of adoration. Beside the goddess that had somehow found time and patience to produce a child, Domina felt like a cement worker from Poggibonsi.

'First tell me about you,' she asked. 'Why didn't you let us know you were coming?'

'Have you forgotten the date?'

'August the eighth. What about it?'

'Jacoby . . . eh? . . . remember your poor father, uh?'

'Oh God, how awful! I'd completely forgotten.' Every year Isobella had made sure she was in the country for the anniversary of Jacoby's coronary so that she could clean his tombstone and honour it with flowers. For the past three years she had been in the country already, so that no issue had been made of the thing. Domina winced from the shame. 'But you should have reminded me,' she complained. 'It's not fair to me to test me like that. You know how absent-minded I can be. And it's not fair to you. Where are you staying? Are you in an hotel?'

'I have an enchanting room in Claridges. This afternoon we'll drive over to Sussex to pay our respects, tonight you're coming to Covent Garden with me – Te Kanawa and Pavarotti, *cara* – then tomorrow you come shopping with me and we fly home on the three o'clock flight.'

'I'll come to the Opera with you, and of course I'll come to Sussex, but I'm not going home.'

'But Domina, I fail to understand you. Randolph has thrown you out; it would be a disgrace to be found skulking here like some sentimental hussy.'

'Randy hasn't thrown me out, Mamma.'

'He hasn't?' The disappointment on Isobella's face fairly sang.

'How did you find out where I was?'

'Well, I arrived in Heathrow yesterday. I looked around. No one to meet me but I think, "That doesn't matter, they're both busy young people." So I went to a *telefono* and rang your Clifton number. That Randolph answered and he said . . . he said . . .' Isobella's face burst into a crinkling laugh. 'He said that you had gone to be with your poor dear mother who was oh so very sick, if not dying in Tuscany. So I waited a bit to get over the shock of being told that I'm very sick and I said, "Randolph, this *is* her mother and I'm neither sick nor *nella bella Toscana*, I'm in beastly Heathrow. Where is my daughter?" Well, at first he didn't want to tell, and I could see that you'd had a row or something, so I said that if he didn't tell me where you were I'd come and stay with him for *weeks*.' She laughed her finely-tuned laugh. 'And he panicked at *that*, I can tell you, and he give me the number of your agent, that lesbian potato.'

'Des isn't a lesbian.'

'Well, she look like one. Anyway, I ring your Desbian and I say I must have your address as it's a matter of life and death.'

'I'll sack her.'

'No, *cara*, don't do that. She is plain and means no harm, and I was so very convincing.'

'Mamma, I haven't had a row with Randolph. I know you can't wait to see us split up but you'll just simply have to wait a little longer, OK?'

'Then why are you living in this slum?'

'Because I was never allowed to before.'

'But you never asked. I'm sure we could have arranged . . .'

'That's just the point. It would have been an arrangement; a tasteful conversion in Islington. I'd had enough of that at the Paragon . . .'

'There. I told you. Randolph is the end.'

'No, not Randolph – comfort, luxury. I could feel myself getting dull. I'm on a kind of holiday. It's a sort of rest-cure for my work.'

'You're collecting material *here*? Why don't you just watch it on your soap operas? This – *c'e spaventole, veramente vulgaro*. Your father, God forgive his soul, perhaps he would have understood – he was sometimes the British eccentric like this – but I, I cannot see it. You think it's just for art, but it's snobbish too, you know that?'

'What?'

'It's snobbish, I said. You think you can sail into a place like this and write about them all as if they were merely characters for your stage, but they're people, Domina, real people, and if they found out what you're doing they'd be most upset.'

'Oh, Mamma, *really*. You don't know what it's like. They don't know who I am. No one ever does, not these sort of people anyway. If I were Fi Templeton, perhaps they might – they remember actresses – but me? Never. They think Domina Feraldi is a luscious Italian.'

'Well, so she is. Half of her.'

'I am glad you're here, Mamma. You look wonderful.'

Isobella chuckled and shook her daughter's chin in a familiar gesture. The frank sexiness of that chuckle had always come as a pleasant surprise.

'I'm glad I'm here, too. It's so good to have you on your *own*! Now I must go and pay some calls. You'll meet me for lunch, of course. If you come to my room I'll have something sent up, then we can set out for Sussex in good time. *Va bene?*'

'*Va bene, Mamma. A l'una.*'

They kissed and Isobella insisted she see herself out. No daughter of hers would be seen wandering through a slum in a state of *déshabillé*. Domina returned to her room, saw Avril Gilchrist's manuscript on the floor, and remembered that she had quite forgotten to telephone Westminster Bureau the night before. Already excited at the day off sweet Fate had granted her, she took a ten-pence piece and hurried down to call them now to apologize and announce that she would not be available for work until Friday.

13

Domina paused half-way up the staircase. Someone had left the naked light bulb burning over the pay-phone. Exhilarated by Italian and duty-free brandy, she swayed, staring into the pool of light. It was late but she knew he'd be awake. She stepped forward and dug a coin from her bag. She mouthed the familiar digits as she dialled. The moment the pips finished she was embarrassed at the clarity with which her voice pealed out in the stairwell.

'Randy? It's the paramour. Did I wake you? . . . Good . . . Oh, I'm fine. Thanks for the letter. Des forwarded it to me . . . Mamma did? . . . Yes, I know. She turned up this morning and found me still in bed . . . No, it wasn't your fault. It was nice to see her, anyway. We went to Sussex this afternoon and I've just got back from the Opera . . . It's the eighth – Daddy's grave . . . Yes . . . No, I'm fine, honestly. How are you? Oh blast! No more change . . . I . . . Yes . . . I love you too. 'Bye.'

The pips cut her off and she said 'bye to the bald dialling tone. She switched off the light, continued up to the attic, and wished she had not rung him. Mamma and she had spent the evening playing wised-up women of the world, wry sybils of the Mother Goddess, and now she had let the side down.

Quintus Harding was playing his Gregorian chant

again. She tried to get past it, came as far as sliding her key into the lock, then turned and knocked at his door.

'Who is it?'

'It's ... it's Mrs Tey. Can I come in?' Footsteps approached the door and he let her in. She saw at once that he had been working. The room was dark save for a lamp on a table in the window where several books lay open. 'Oh, I am sorry. You're working.'

'Yes,' he said, 'but it doesn't matter.'

'No.' She felt drunk. Gross. 'I mustn't disturb you. It was only the music. I heard it the other night. The nuns used to sing something like it at school. It's something I can never quite shake off.'

'Come in and listen properly.'

'No. You must get on with your reading. This is the *Regina Coeli*, isn't it?'

'That's right. Look, do come in. I wasn't concentrating in any case.'

She found herself sitting on the edge of his bed while he shut the door behind her and returned to his seat at the table. He had no curtains, and she could see that the red geraniums she had seen from the road were his. The room had an academic air, like someone's sitting room in College.

'You must have a marvellous view,' she said.

'Not really.'

'Well, it's better than mine. Can you see the Gardens?'

'Just about. Well, some of the trees. But it's noisier than a back room during the day. And that sign gets on my nerves.'

'Which?'

'The Hermes one. I think something's the matter with it. It's been flickering like that for weeks now.'

Domina stood to follow his gaze down into the street to the crippled flashing of the blue neon letters.

'Oh. That place. It's a sauna, isn't it?'

'Sort of. Thierry goes there a lot. He made me come with him once, but I find that sort of heat gives me a headache.' He had been playing with a pencil which now snapped. 'Damn!' he exclaimed. 'Oh. Sorry. Have you been out?'

'Yes. My mother's in town and she had seats for Convent Garden. *Traviata*.'

'Good?'

'Marvellous. Pavarotti and Kiri Te Kanawa.'

'Not really my kind of thing,' he started, but the Gregorian chant came to an end and he moved to deal with it. Domina stood.

'Now I must go to bed and let you get on with your reading.' The room made her unaccountably tense.

'No. Please stay. Unless you're exhausted, that is. I've been reading non-stop since about eight and my head's fit to burst. Only if you're not tired, though.'

She sat down again without a word. She noticed the icon over his pillow. An old, haloed man clutching a haloed boy to his side and leaning on a staff. A lily was flowering on the top of the latter and a dove floated overhead.

'That's Saint Joseph, isn't it?' she said.

'It's copied from one of the side altars at Santa Sofia. Can I put on something else now? I hate talking over chant.'

'No. I mean, yes do, and no it doesn't feel quite right, does it?'

He laughed, then checked himself. It was a trait she had noticed when they were talking in the Gardens, before she had fled and left him dealing with the keeper and the goose; he never allowed his laughs to die a natural death, but choked them. He put on some unaccompanied Bach. A cello suite. Randy had been trying to make her listen to unaccompanied Bach for twenty years, but it made her laugh, which made him cross. As Quintus returned to his seat by the window she wondered whether she was going to laugh now. The gravity with which he evidently took himself would be ludicrous were it not for the sneaking suspicion, aroused once more as his features were brushed by the light of the lamp, that he was rather good-looking. Good-looking in a hopeless, ascetic way, of course.

'Why Saint Joseph?' she asked. 'Isn't there a Saint Quintus?'

'No. Irredeemably Latin, I'm afraid. Besides, I've never held with the idea of revering a saint simply because you share their name. Parents can't tell whether children will grow up to find their namesakes relevant. You can't emulate to order. There has to be some sympathetic desire. No, I chose dear Saint Joseph. Or perhaps he chose me.'

'Why?'

'He's always appealed. I felt terribly sorry for him at first, no spectacular martyrdom, just self-effacement.'

'But he'd been married before, hadn't he?'

'You can't be sure. The part about him being an old man was patently invented by the artists and translators to ease the discomfort of the situation. Especially in Italy. They just couldn't bear to contemplate that kind of wilful emasculation. Being cuckolded by God seems less unjust if you tell yourself that he's past his prime, that it's a second marriage, and turn him into a protective father figure with a wispy beard.'

'Do you want to emulate his peaceful death?'

'Don't mock,' he said, frowning.

'Sorry. I'm not really. I just think it's a little premature to attach yourself to the patron saint of the deathbed.'

'He's a hero of male chastity, too. At least, he is to my mind.'

To Domina's mind the two were one – celibacy, a cripple's existence.

'Why Quintus, then? Were you actually number five?'

'Yes. Well, fifth born. There were twins the year before me who only lived a couple of hours.'

'Oh, how terrible! Your poor mother.' She wanted to ask him how it felt to grow up with a name that was an abiding reminder of death. The mother must be sick. 'How old are the other two?'

'Much older. Roderick's thirty-two – he's a vet – and Jennifer's thirty.'

So you were the baby, she thought. 'I was an only child,' she confessed.

'I know.'

'How?'

'Because you ask so many questions.'

'Sorry.'

'No. That sounded rude. It's nice to have someone to chat to.'

'Don't you talk to the rest of them?'

'Not much. They come and go so often that it seems rather a waste of effort getting to know them.'

'But Penny and Avril?'

'Penny seems to be scared of me. I can never make her relax. Avril's quite sweet.'

'And what about Thierry?'

'Oh ... well ... things have always been a bit difficult there.' His voice sank and he abruptly started shutting books. Even in the half-light his blush could be seen, unexpected on his bloodless cheeks. 'Where did you get to like Gregorian chant?' he went on. She stopped staring and played with her dress.

'At school. Saint Mary's, Clanworth.'

'I thought that was a Catholic convent.'

'It was. My mother's Italian.'

'But you ...'

'I married into a Church of England cathedral close. Talk about the pork pie at the Jewish wedding.' The joke was suspiciously out of character; she ought to be in bed. He laughed, though, then checked himself.

'When did your husband ... ?'

'Last year.'

'Oh. I'm sorry.'

'Not at all. Why are you reading history books? I thought, when you mentioned your Brother Jerome ...'

'Oh. That's strictly unofficial. As far as my parents are concerned, I'm a second year historian at UCL. I discovered the cathedral quite by accident.'

'Which cathedral?'

'Santa Sofia's. It's the Greek Orthodox one by the Moscow Road, down there. Well, it wasn't quite accidental. I'm specializing in the Ottoman Empire, Eastern church powers and things. One day last spring, it must have been, I was buying cakes in the Moscow Road bakery and got inquisitive and went inside. It struck me I ought to know just what Orthodoxy was all about. I went home to dump the cakes, and came back in time for the next service.'

'And now you're hooked.'

'Let's just say I'm convinced.'

The firmness of his tone disturbed her. It was so unlike the bland security of the Christian Unionists at Cambridge. It dawned on her that they had been the last young believers she had met.

'Why the classes with Brother Jerome?' she dared.

'Well, to start with I just went to ask him to explain things. I'd had a standard C of E childhood – christening, Sunday School, scripture classes, confirmation and no awkward questions allowed. The services are mostly in English (and anyway I've got a bi-lingual prayer book) but I felt an outsider. I felt I was enjoying them for the wrong reasons: the music, the smells, the vague sense that here were some people with convictions. I started just talking to Jerome about fundamentals of their belief – still very much the roving historian – then I realized that I was getting ready for something bigger.'

'You wanted to convert to Orthodoxy?'

'More than that.' He gave out a sharp little laugh. 'I think I might want to become a monk.'

'God! I mean, goodness.' Her mind reeled. This was obscene. 'Do your parents have no idea at all?'

'None.'

'Wouldn't they be upset?'

'They wouldn't understand, so yes, I suppose they would be.'

'What do they want you to do?'

'They don't want me to specialize in History. They don't dare say that, because they don't ever show how stupid they are, but I've mentioned that possibility and I could feel them disapproving.'

'Why? What does your father do?'

'He's retired now. He was in the RAF. That's his only link with me.'

'You don't want to join . . .'

'No. But I fly.'

Biggles in sackcloth. She really must go to bed.

'You fly? Where did you learn to do that?'

'They were so keen, they sent me to Braddleton instead of somewhere more Oxbridge orientated.'

'I thought that was Army.'

'Guns. Boats. Planes. Horses. Cricket. Rugger. Anything but Oxbridge.'

'Or the Ottoman Empire. Were you miserable?'

'At first. Then I realized how nice it was to be miles from home and started joining in with things. I've got twenty-twenty vision so they put me in the RAF division of the Corps and I learnt how to fly. Got my licence before I left. God knows why, really. I knew I'd never want to be a pilot or fight or anything.'

'But it must be wonderful. I know that sounds crass, but . . . well – flying! Sorry. It's only that it's so utterly unexpected. Do you ever get a chance now?'

'Oh yes. I go every week. Sundays. You must come up.'

'Is that allowed?' She could barely contain her excitement.

'Of course. I've got my advanced licence now, and I'm fully insured.'

'Where do you fly?'

'Biggin Hill.'

'Oh, of course.' The gigue bounced to a close and the cello suite was over. Domina yawned. 'Sorry. How desperately rude of me.'

'Not at all.'

'My mother appeared on the doorstep at dawn and it's been a long, long day.' She rose and started for the door. 'I must let you get some sleep. Thanks so much for putting up with me. I think I was . . .'

'No. It was lovely.'

' . . . I was just feeling rather homesick all of a sudden.' It simply came out. She blushed and put her hand on the door.

'Wait a second.' He jumped up. His voice was so very young and eager. She turned. He was unrolling a poster. 'Look. Isn't it marvellous? I found it today. There was a sale on in Poster Warehouse. I've been wanting to get one of this for ages, but they've always been so small. This is *huge* – look!' He unrolled the poster along the top of the bed. It was nearly six feet high and four feet wide. The writing was in Dutch, or something Low. It was Brueghel's *The Fall of Icarus*.

'It's wonderful,' she said, but had always found it sinister; like enjoying a picnic in a poppy-waving meadow, then discovering that you've been eating beside a dead cow. 'It's so big. You can see everything.'

'Exactly. I thought it could go up there, on that wall opposite the window. It's ten times larger than the real thing, I'm sure. Just look at the detail. It's funny, in the first week of knowing Brother Jerome, we discovered that we both liked it for the same reason.'

'What?'

'The perfect martyrdom. Quiet, like Saint Joseph's. The workers in the fields, the sailors in the sea, even the birds and the animals – they're all carrying on as though nothing was happening. Icarus has given his life to a dream, to trying to reach the sun, and he's falling so beautifully. I know it's morbid and sounds stupid but the picture feels frozen. Of course all pictures are frozen, but, oh I'm not explaining this properly.' She watched his eyes flicker across the paper. 'It's as if he'd wanted to paint the *silence*, to hold that moment when Icarus starts to plummet down and just before anyone has noticed. It's the instant, just there, when his death has a meaning, when he's altered the whole landscape.'

Domina struggled to think of something to say, but she'd been concentrating on his eyes and lips and could only sigh, smile. She broke the moment by straightening up. It was as if she had checked his laughter. At once he was adolescent again, awkward, self-effacing. He stooped and started to roll up the poster.

'You shouldn't let me ramble on like this. You must go to bed.'

14

'*Cum veni Sancti Spiritu.*' The children's voices were as bright as the glass in the cupola whence the sunlight fell to the black and white checks of the marble floor. The light gave substance to the rich fragrance that spilled from the swinging censers. There was a congregation of souls but they were behind. Sister Charity (games) was as lovely as she had remembered her. The oval face. The almond eyes. The long, long body and the voice, '*Veni mecum, sanctissima ancilla Domina Sofia Feraldi. Dominus tecum est. Veni mecum Domina Feraldi ad magistrum amoris.*' Sister Charity spoke through a smile, and extended a perfect hand. Domina took it, still hugging her Debrett's to her naked chest. Together they waded through the arum lilies, down the avenue of altar boys. The boys were swinging censers and tossing handfuls of sugared almonds, exquisite, pink, blue and pearly white, from that little shop outside Saint Sulpice.

'And lighten with celestial fire, da deedle dumti da deedle dum,' *les enfants chantent.* The almonds tapped her lightly all over, on her breasts, her thighs, her back. Some caught in her ankle-length hair, and stayed there, eggs in a nest.

They reached the high altar and Sister Charity was taking away Debrett's, oh so softly, her fingernails barely touching Domina's skin as she did so. And now she was holding out a goose. It was a Canada goose, and it was dead. She lifted its head back and presented Domina with the lifeless breast. '*Osculi avem amoris*,' she commanded.

'Pavarotti Crush Bar and give her back a scrub down, like,' Ginny called from behind her cello.

Domina bent forward and sank her lips into the down. The angelus bells jangled and the bird shook out its wings and was gone.

'Oh Christ, Dad, she's not dead, Dad, she's not dead!'

Sister Charity turned back from the altar once more holding up a gnarled wooden staff, only now she was Mamma.

'Kiss it, *cara*. Go on. Kiss God's rod.' Domina bent and kissed. The angelus sounded again and she looked up to see green shoots sprout forth from the tip of the rod, shoots that opened out into lilies, freesia, montana, a cluster of white waxy blooms. She knew she had to walk on now, past the fluttering lace of the altar boys, past the high altar, which by now was the size of a Chippendale writing desk. Mamma Carita (games) was instructing a small Japanese maid. '*E dica al ragazzo di lasciare il conto sul tavolo della cucina*,' she said. '*Vado prima al salone di belleza. Diamine! Ancora il telefono.*'

Watched by the congregation of souls, Domina came out into the sunny field where the bi-plane was waiting. She knew that the sweets had melted all over her skin into circles of damp confetti.

He was standing inside, in white kid. He waved a gloved hand and threw her a penetrating smile. She felt herself grow hot in the face. A vast black woman was scrubbing the wheels. As Domina approached, she presented her glossy back as a stool. 'You're the Boss, missy,' she laughed, 'remember, you's the Boss.'

Poised with one naked leg on the seat and one on the cleaner's back, with his smile on her breasts and the air piping with the squabbling of sparrows, Domina told herself, 'This is very Ecstasy.'

15

The propeller was a roaring blur, a hail of sugared almonds was pelting over her skin, her legs were about his neck and truly this is the meaning of bliss, she thought.

But the bi-plane couldn't move away. It would start forward, then be tugged back, start forward, then be tugged back. The lurching sickened Domina and she turned to see the black woman clinging to the tail-end, her face contorted with glistening rage.

'What? What time?' Domina murmured.

'Phone. Mrs Tey? Here, there's a phone call for you!'

Eight o'clock. Domina threw back the sheets and ran, half-awake, out to the landing.

'Here. Phone call,' gargled Mrs Moorhouse and launched into a very wet cough.

Bridget Croak, remembered Domina. Bridget Croak, the fat frog housekeeper in that Racey Helps book.

'Hello?'

'Domina. Hello there. It's Jo.'

'Oh. Hi.' Who was Jo?

'You said you'd be free today, yes?'

'Oh. Yes.'

'Great. We've got a job for you. Copy typist stroke clerk, bank in Holborn, nine to five-thirty, three-fifty an hour, starting today and carrying on until at least next Friday. Sound OK?'

'Perfect.'

'Fantastic. Have you got a pencil there?'

'Yup,' she lied.

'Well, it's the Hagushiri Banking Corporation, Shanghai House, Holborn. Just report at Reception and they'll send someone down to find you. Can't miss it. It's a big tower up in the two hundreds on the left. How are you on tubes?'

'Fine.'

'Great. Look forward to hearing how you get on. Call in here on your way home and we'll give you a time sheet. Pay's a week in arrears.'

''Bye.'

'*Ciao.*'

'Hagushiri, Shanghai House, Holborn. Hagushiri, Shanghai House, Holborn. Hagushiri, shit shit shit, Shanghai House,' Domina muttered under her breath as she raced back into her room and scrabbled for a pencil and paper.

Mr Punjabi was in the bath singing selections from the Andrews Sisters' repertoire, so by the time she descended the basement steps, fragrant, impeccably turned out, in need of strong black coffee to still a churning stomach, it was five to nine.

'*Comment, Domina? Est-ce que tu dois te confesser déjà?*'

'Hello, Thierry. No, I've got to go to work and I'm late and it's my first day and I don't want to go.'

'Have my coffee. I haven't touched it and it'll be cooler.'

'Bless you.' She accepted the mug and took a deep gulp. Thierry spooned some more grounds into the percolator and let out a heavy sigh. '*Mais qu'est-ce que tu as?*' she asked.

'*Mon ange est parti.*'

'Billy? Oh dear.'

'His name was Dwight.'

'Yes. Dwight. He had such a sweet smile.'

'That's the way. I think you English call it "Sod's Law"; *ça veut dire*, perfection, if and when you find it, is always accounted for or about to board a plane for Newark, New Jersey.'

'Which was he?'

'*Tous les deux.* You're late for work. You must go.'

She took the Central Line. The carriage was full. A baby was yelling close by. She wanted to slap it. She had to stand with one arm in the air. The man with the greasy forehead, who shared her metal pole, seemed to have chewed a head of garlic for breakfast.

At Tottenham Court Road almost all the girls left the carriage. Domina took an itchy seat. The garlic man, who had sat down opposite her in the seat for disabilities and heavy shopping, fumbled in a pocket of his brown suit and produced a half-eaten Mars bar. He peeled the black paper away to reveal the point where he had left off, and took a large bite. Nougat crumbs spilled onto his tie and a washing-line of caramel dangled, snapped, then clung to the contour of his chin. Domina looked away. Smile when you introduce yourself, and remember to shake hands. The importance of first appearances cannot be overstressed. Every temporary is an ambassador for Westminster Bureau.

She emerged, flushed, on to the sunny pavement. Her eyes felt as tight as a pig's. She wavered, obstructing the purpose of passers-by, while trying to relate what she saw to the square of the A to Z she remembered. She struck out along Holborn. Once she succeeded in finding a building with a number, she realized that she was at quite the wrong end of the street. She quickened her pace. Her scalp began to itch with the salt of surfacing sweat. She glanced at her watch. It was nearly half-past nine. Saint Paul's appeared in view. She stepped off the pavement and had to leap backwards into the crowd as a van bore honking down on her. One of her heels wobbled threateningly.

'Don't worry,' said a man with kipper tie and scarlet face, 'it may never happen.'

She brayed almost wildly in the teeth of his perky smile and set off once more. How could people do this for a living?

One hundred and three. One hundred and five. One hundred and seven. The numbers stopped. She passed the base of a glass and chrome office block. A stitch began to wrench at her ribs. Another door. Another number. The number was three. It should have been one hundred and eleven but the number was three. The stitch brought Domina to a standstill.

'Oh, bloody hell!' she exclaimed, and leant against the nearest wall to regain her breath. A bus crawling up from Saint Paul's made up her mind. Dumping the Total Temping Package in a bin, she wove her way between the cars to the next stop and raised a hand.

A thrill of nostalgia hummed through her as she tapped across the polished floor of the loggia. Sister Annunciata had obtained permission for her to work in Senate House library in the summer before her Oxbridge term. The place lent a cinematic glamour to dogged hard work; an effect of the Mussolini-meets-Caligula look. Trooping in with the ashen-faced finalists each morning, she had imagined herself an extra in *Metropolis*. Standing again in a great steel lift, clutching a virgin notebook and the dog-eared envelope she had suddenly started to scribble on in the top of the bus, Domina felt the sweet familiar buzz. Whenever this sensation came upon her, she perceived afresh that her work was a serious addiction.

'Hello, I'd like a day ticket, please, so I could use the Periodicals Room.'

'Are you a student?' The attendant gave her a quizzical once-over.

'Yes. At Bristol,' Domina lied, and handed over an English Faculty Library ticket one of Randy's students had left behind once.

'Fine,' said the uniformed woman, copying out a slip. 'One day ticket, for the twentieth, for Miss Cary McNichol. There we are. The Periodicals Room's through there, where they're stamping out books, through the doors at the end, past the display cases then turn sharp right.'

Domina shied away from any attempt to make her discuss her modes of composition. She found the concept of inspiration embarrassing because it was so near the truth and yet so high-flown and irrational. Her imagination had always been a vivid one but she had been blessed with a childhood in which grown-ups smiled and dubbed her an incorrigible story-teller, rather than slapping her wrist and telling her not to lie. She held that the spicing of conversation with undetected untruths was a priceless social art form. The spinning out of exchanges between characters was thus no more taxing than entertaining her cleaning-woman, and therefore only mildly entertaining for herself. The thrill lay in plotting. The ideas tended to come during conjunctions of manual occupation with mental vacancy. She would be clipping roses, scraping her feet with a pumice stick, once she had been making jam, when the seeds of a plot arrived. There was never any preliminary concentration on the matter, they simply 'arrived'; hence the embarrassment concerning inspiration. Had she been a poetess, or even poor Rick, had she been a writer of sub-Strindberg, the awkwardness would have been less. The difficulty was that her medium was Middle-Class Domestic, and Thalia tended to do her stuff during bouts of middle-class domesticity; one could never own to the agency of pumice sticks and sugar thermometers. Her advocates believed each play to be a feat of cerebral engineering from conception onwards and she would not deceive them.

Once the ideas had come there was no danger of losing them altogether, but from the moment of their arrival there were offshoots and fleetingly suggested developments that had to be recorded as they came to her. By twelve-thirty she had the bare bones before her. A librarian aged thirty-nine, called Fay Harker, has been living all her life with her draconian mother who acts as secretary to the bishop of an important northern diocese. Driven by the demand that she mind the bring-and-buy stall at yet another Uganda Mission coffee morning and by the realization that should she accept the choir-master's proposal it will be out of sheer bloody-mindedness, she grabs her savings and runs away. She moves into a bedsit in an extravagantly seedy building in West London where she pretends to be the widow of a canon. Against the background of street fighting and general social unrest, she becomes involved with a young priest who has moved into the house in a spirit of charitable Evangelism, and proceeds to summon up the considerable worldly passion which neither party knew they could muster.

As morning mellowed into afternoon, Domina began to lose concentration and to brood. The hairdresser had said she looked only thirty. Sitting in this roomful of students brought home to her just how easy it was to *feel* twenty-five. Or was it that she felt like a twenty-five-year-old? Increasingly, she let her stare drift up from her pad to her neighbours. At the table opposite, a girl was poring over her *Browning Quarterly*, a wholly inappropriate smirk playing about her lips. The boy across the table from her was sitting back in his chair, hands in pockets. He was smirking too, his eyes on the girl's face as though willing her to giggle. Domina took off her reading glasses to get a better look.

He was well-built – she could see that through his rugger shirt. There was a fleck of mud on his temple. He had taken a copy of *Sound and Vision* off the shelves and propped it open on a stand before him. She wasn't fooled. 'Meet you after my match,' he had written, 'four o'clock, Periodicals Room, table eight.' Then Domina saw why they were smirking. Only one of his feet was on the floor. An empty shoe lay beside it. He shifted his thighs slightly and the girl let out a gasp that was turned into a cough.

Domina flipped her pad shut, threw it with her pen into her bag, and made for the lifts. She would go out with a young man. She had to go out with a young man.

16

A hot, oily bath, some hours and several fortifying gins later, she was led out of the front door by Thierry.

'I thought this was a men-only sauna,' she said, as he swept her past the neon sign, up the steps and into the red-lit hall. A large woman whose quantities of gold glistered behind the reception desk chuckled aloud as she saw them.

'Evening, Terry, love,' he said. 'One and a guest; that's two-fifty. Hello, dearie. Haven't seen you before.'

'No,' said Domina, twitching. 'Hello. Thierry, let me, please.'

'My responsibility, my treat,' said Thierry. 'Come on.'

She followed him into the thickening crimson gloom. What she could see of the walls was hung with thick flock paper. The hellish glow overthrew all colour distinction.

'I suppose the red is to hide the bloodstains on the stair-carpet,' she joked.

'*Comment?*'

'Nothing.'

As they descended the basement stairs, the temperature rose sharply. There was a smell of gin and cigarettes, laced with sweat and stale Eau Sauvage. A disco beat was thudding steadily nearer. They reached another reception desk. By the light of a piece of reproduction Art Deco, a moustachioed lavatory brush smiled in welcome. He stubbed out his cigarette in an ashtray shaped like an outstretched hand. In her hasty glance, Domina noticed a magenta stain around the stub.

'Hello, you old slag. Welcome back to the Herpes. Who's your lady friend, then?'

'That's my secret.' Thierry turned to her, '*C'est vraiment dégueulasse.*'

'Where's your tickets, then?'

'There you are, Percy.'

'You know that's not my name,' said the brush and swung round to Domina, lifting his eyes to heaven. 'Thinks she's *that* sharp, does our Tel.' Domina grinned sheepishly, and glanced behind her. A small queue was forming. All men. She wondered how often Gerald came here. Their host continued, 'There's your towels. Pink for a prissy little girl.' He handed Thierry a towel. It had 47 embroidered on one corner. 'And blue for Madam.'

'Thank you so much.' Domina took hers and hurried after Thierry who was disappearing down a corridor to their right. After the glare of the lamp, the darkness was blinding. There were occasional puddles on the floor. She heard the waver in her voice as she called after him. 'Thierry? Thierry, I thought you said it wasn't *really* a sauna. I can't very well . . . Why did he give us . . . ?' She almost fell over his slight frame in the dark. Where he had stopped, a thin rectangle of red light defined a closed door.

'This is the only hard part,' he assured her. 'You must simply keep walking. It's usually very crowded, so hold onto my belt.'

'What? Why?' she blurted, with a feeble gesture of blue towel number forty-eight, but he thrust open the door.

She snatched hold of his belt out of pure terror and was

towed into the engulfing clouds of steam. The disco music was suddenly all around them; an aggressive woman wailing, 'Eight hundred guys, and you bet I'm gonna gonna need 'em now!'

The shelves and walls were lined with shining male flesh. Men milled everywhere, clad only in the miasma of steam and hot body. They made no attempt to make way for Thierry. She was glad she had a hold on his belt, the impulse to let herself fall into the crowd was akin to feeling one can fly off a cliff top. A brazier glowed to one side. Someone ladled water onto it as she passed, and the sudden hiss caused her to jump. When they emerged into the unexpected room on the other side, she found herself gleaming with sweat. Never had twenty paces taken so long.

The first thing she recognized was a bar. She walked straight over, sat on a stool and ordered two double gin and tonics.

'Towels get you your first drink free,' said the barman, taking her towel and serving her.

Grinning, understanding her predicament exactly, Thierry perched to her left, accepted his drink with nodded thanks, and waited for her to recover. She downed half hers in gulps, staring at the rows of bottles and postcards from Ibiza and San Diego, then pulled a handkerchief from her sleeve to mop her brow before swivelling around to face Thierry and the subterranean bar.

'Lion, the Witch and the bloody Wardrobe,' she muttered.

'*Comment?*'

'Never mind. Is this place legal?' she went on, trying not to stare too obviously.

'*Mais bien sûr, Minou.*'

'Sorry. Do I look so very new?' Talking French was protective and she started to relax. 'It's just so unexpected.'

The room, which was cavernous, appeared to continue around the corner underneath the neighbouring house. The ceiling arched like a wine cellar. Shabbily grandiose blue and gold curtains dangled onto a stage at the other end from the bar. Around the walls were ranged niches, formed by pairs of what could have been seats from some 1918 railway carriage. The 'period' feel was continued in the heavy plush swathing of the lamps at each table. Even the jukebox had a neo-Edwardian casing. The place was filling fast. Men outnumbered women at a rate of fifty to one.

'Apparently it used to be a somewhat disreputable restaurant,' said Thierry, 'but no one can remember that. It's all perfectly legal. Kevin – that's the monster who sold us the tickets – he runs it as a members-only club, but that's a formality. The sauna keeps out the uninitiated.'

'That I can well believe.'

'So what do you think?'

'It's mad,' she said, starting to distinguish a few fairly attractive individuals from the swelling crowd. 'I think I like it. Is it always this busy?'

'This is nothing. You wait till later.'

'It's quite late already.'

'After the show the licence runs out and they go on to fruit juice and Perrier. That's when it gets busy. All the ones who've had no luck come on here when the pubs close.'

'What show?' She had to raise her voice across the

shoulders of a blond youth of thirty-five who had pushed through to the bar between them.

'There's always a show. It's a cabaret club.'

'But that's marvellous! I had no idea. What kind? Singing?'

'Not exactly.' He grinned as he looked at his watch. 'It should be starting soon. Hey, Flo!' he lapsed into English and called to the barman, 'Flo, what's on the menu tonight, my darling?'

'*Three's a Crowd*, so help us God,' he called back. 'Who's your lady friend, then?'

'Just a girl from Scotland Yard.'

'Oh, ha fucking ha.'

'Are you sure I'm not cramping your style?' Domina asked.

'*Pas du tout*,' Thierry reassured her. 'In the land of the walking dead, a little novelty is all too welcome.'

'But look, if you . . . I mean, well. If you . . .'

'If I see anyone I like, I swear I'll tell you to bugger off.'

'Thanks,' she laughed. The jukebox was playing a Dusty Springfield song to which she used to fornicate. She sang along in an undertone. Her voice was breathy and low, 'I close my eyes and count to ten, and when I open them you're still there . . .'

'Don't tell me this was your era?' he jeered. 'I had no idea you were so ancient.'

'I used to snog to this.'

'A woman of affairs?'

'No. But . . .'

'I want to know what your first real boyfriend looked like.'

'Would it turn you on?' She surmised that no one had told him about poor, late Paul.

'Well,' he said, 'I can't have you, so it's the next best thing.' Domina mentally undressed his wiry Breton body, and though he was short, couldn't see why not. 'You must tell me if you see someone you like, then I shall go say how do you do. As you say in English, other people's people is my "thing".'

'What happened when you brought poor Quintus here?' she asked, deciding that mischief deserved mischief.

'Did he tell you about it?'

'Not exactly, but I guessed.'

'I was wild about him, darling – the vulnerable appeal of the startled colt. I thought he just needed leading out. I guess this wasn't the place to lead him.'

'Was it a complete disaster?'

'A *débâcle*. Fiasco.' He shrugged his shoulders. 'How was I to know he was a religious maniac?'

'What happened?'

'Not much. He ran. Just ran off to pray for my salvation, I expect.'

'Poor thing.'

'Him or *moi*?'

'Him of course; *you* can obviously look after yourself.'

'So very depressing.'

'What? Being a survivor?'

'Yes. I have my little crises but no one ever thinks to worry. Sometimes one misses a mother's love.'

As he chattered on, ginfully analysing his psychosexual fate, Domina saw Randy. He was leaning up against the opposite wall, staring at her companion. He had the same thick black hair, the same nose, same jaw, same stance. Even the clothes could have been his. It struck her, gazing at his replica, that it had never crossed her mind that her lover might be bisexual, no more than it had ever occurred to her to look in other women for anything but competition. Another man as a rival in his affections would be impossible to bear; he would lack all the usual points of comfortable comparison.

'Thierry?' she asked.

'What's the matter? You're staring like a madwoman.'

'He looks just like an amazing ex of mine. No. Not yet. Turn round slowly in a moment. He's over there by the wall. Behind you. In the old leather jacket. Curly, black hair. Jewish sort of nose.'

'I can see him in the mirror,' he said. 'Saint Catherine keep you, my child.' With practised disregard he slid from his stool. 'As that Scottish hero of yours said, I may be taking some time.'

He walked over to the jukebox which had fallen silent a moment before and set it playing. Sinatra. *Strangers in the Night*. Then, with a waver of a smile to Domina, he turned and leant against the machine. She marvelled at the way he met 'Randy's' following gaze so calmly.

They stared, boy and man, almost without breaking, for some three minutes. She spectated Wimbledon fashion. Then Thierry flashed him a radiant smile, and looked bashfully to the stage, where the curtains were showing signs of life. Her heart sprang to her mouth as 'Randy' drained his whisky glass and walked straight over to him. He touched Thierry on the shoulder, Thierry turned to face him, they exchanged a few words, Randy set the jukebox playing the disco song she had heard in the sauna, and they proceeded to kiss. The embrace lasted some minutes. All she could see of Thierry were his hands as they kneaded and scratched at the back of the leather jacket.

'Never seen *that* in the flicks, have you?'

She started, embarrassed. Flo was grinning at her. She had been staring.

'No,' she laughed. 'Oh dear. Was I staring?'

'Nothing odd about staring in a place like this. You'd be unpopular if you didn't. You live near here, then?'

'Not far. Actually, that reminds me. I ought to be getting home.'

'Oh. Won't you stay for the show?'

'Well, I'm awfully tired.'

'And you don't want to be a gooseberry. Now *you* are a very tactful, sensible girl,' he said. 'So you won't be walking young Tel home, then?'

'I think,' she said, 'I think he can look after himself.'

'I'll say nightie-night for you, if you like.'

'Would you?'

'No hassle.' He broke off to serve a couple. 'You both staying in the same place, then?' he resumed. 'Over at Lady Tilly's?'

'That's right.'

'Tell you what, then.' On reflection, Flo bore more than a passing resemblance to Aunt Juliana-Costanza – a seedier version, of course. 'I'll tell him to ring your bell as he comes in, if he needs rescuing.'

'That would be sweet of you. He's probably fine, but I can't help . . .'

'Just can't help worrying. Don't I know it. I have to

watch this lot every night. I ask you, who'd be a mother, eh?' Flo's ample frame rocked at the thought.

'Flo? It is Flo, isn't it?'

'That's right, love. Everybody's favourite maiden aunt.'

'There isn't another way out, is there?'

'Excitement of the sauna too much for you?'

'Just a little.'

''Course there is, ducky.' He lifted the flap in the bar. 'Come on. Under here.'

Restored to the security of her attic, Domina flopped exhausted on to her bed and pulled off her shoes and tights. Her clothes reeked of cigarettes, which meant that her hair would, too. Her eyes were stinging. She bathed them in cold water. As she brushed her teeth she looked in the mirror and scowled. Introducing . . . the Bloodshot Fag Hag.

As she fell into bed and turned out the light, she remembered Thierry, pressed up against the jukebox by a man he'd never met. She suffered a twinge of jealous guilt. She should never have left him in that place, even if he did go there every night. The man looked awfully nice. Just like Randy. But appearances deceived. There was always the bell. The bell would wake her up. What if he turned nasty after they'd got upstairs? Thierry was young. He couldn't be much more than twenty. Her thoughts twining now around Thierry and his new man, now around the real Randy, then around the work she had started in the library, Domina slid into unconsciousness.

She opened her eyes and stared into the dark.

'Who's that?'

'Please, Domina. Please!' Thierry whispered in strangled English.

Fogged with sleep, she thrust back the sheets and limped to open the door.

'*Dépêche-toi!*'

No sooner was the door ajar than Thierry rushed in and slammed it behind him. He slipped the catch on the lock. He was naked, but appeared not to have noticed. Terror made his face still whiter than usual. He stood there panting, holding up a hand to keep her silent. Then he followed her drifting eyes and snatched up a petticoat.

'*Je m'excuse.*'

'*Je vous en prie*, but what the hell's the matter?'

'Ssh! Please, Domina.'

'Why? What time is it?' Her window was open and the night had made the room cool. She shivered.

'He tried to kill me.'

'Who? Oh my *God*!' She stopped staring and passed him a dressing gown. 'Here.'

'Thank you.'

'How . . . ?'

'Ssh! He's still here.' He looked ludicrously tense; a whippet in Laura Ashley. Such a spectacle at such an hour made her want to laugh. Then she understood. 'I had no idea,' he went on, still in a stage whisper but back in French, 'I brought him back here and we went up to my room and, er, kissed some more, and then suddenly he pulled . . . he pulled a knife on me. Ssh!'

She had been about to sit back on the bed, but something in his terrified expression froze her. There was someone on the stairs. Footsteps ran heavily up the last little flight from Thierry's landing and stopped by the telephone. Domina didn't dare catch Thierry's eye for fear of giggling or letting out a yelp from sheer tension. She stared hard at the pillow and dug her nails into her palms. Whoever it was took a few paces more and stopped just outside her door.

She imagined Randy, not her Randy, but one that had stayed in the Bronx and grown wild and strange. She pictured him crouching there on the landing, flick-knife in hand, ear against the door. She began to feel as though the slightest movement of her body would be heard, and this set her trembling. She remembered the others. What if one of them, unwitting, opened the door and came out to use the bathroom? Presumably the man was a maniac, and once his blood was up, anyone . . . ? Perhaps Avril would come out, or Penny, or, oh my God, Quintus?

Slowly, Domina allowed her gaze to turn on Thierry. He had lowered himself into the armchair. Tears were coursing down his cheeks. One hand was twisting the dressing-gown cord round and back on his fingers. She tried to remember a prayer, if only to occupy her mind, but they were all about mothers, which made her want to cry.

Then, slowly at first, but breaking into a noisy run, the footsteps descended the stairs.

Thierry looked across at her. They stayed still as death until they heard shoes slapping across the hall tiles, and the front door clattering open and then back into place. He was the first to break the hush and he did so in the poised, language school English he sometimes produced.

'Domina Tey. That is the last, indeed the only time you are going to help me choose a husband.'

As they rolled, racked with tight gasps of laughter, she could only raise a trembling hand to point at the floral dressing gown.

17

Hotel Plaza Luchesi
Firenze
Italia
Thursday

Fascinating Creature,

One would seem to be at a desk in the third room
from the left, *piano secundo*, gazing across filthy but
necessarily beloved Arno to Piazalle Michaelangelo.
Fenella would seem to be here too – not quite sure who
followed or encouraged whom. Mean as hell, as one suspected. Never trust a mouth like that, be the paint
never so thick. This by way of thanks for an enchanting evening. Trust saintly neighbour hasn't had you
evicted. You're welcome to Chester Square if he has. Set
of keys with Bernard next door.

Heaps of affec.
Gerald.

The Paragon
Clifton
Bristol 8
Avon
Friday breakfast

Minnie,

I trust Des has forwarded the last letter. I don't expect a reply. That's a lie. I do, but don't feel you have to rush things. It's only Friday, after all; you haven't been gone a week yet. I wouldn't want you to get any false ideas about my writing again so soon. I can guess how delicate a situation you must be in – looking for oneself is kinda wearing (look what happened to Anaïs Nin, love her). I just happened to be at a loose end with no one to talk to. Seamus, as you possibly remember, prefers a brunch of industrial thinner, so it's just me, the toast and the *New York Review*. Sue Sontag can wait till elevenses, I wanna talk to Baby.

Hi there. Great news! Cowper's done, as are all the other biggies. That leaves just the effortless final statement in which my poised prose structures will raise passing herms to the twentieth century (which as we both know is negligible when it comes to literary madness, hallucinogens being such a lousy cheat). Sorry. That was a regular breakfast sentence. I left it in the middle for coffee. I have no news of great moment. Our favourite theatrical lush tottered round last night and finished your Glenfiddich.

And *that* reminds me why I had to write to you. There is some news. Remember a girl called Cary McNichol? You probably don't since I don't often force my students on you. Cary McNichol is the only promising third year I've got. She also wrote a really smart little thesis on Blake's visionary prosody for the prize last year, and happened to go to my old high school, which is why I've always had, well, a kind of soft spot

114

for her. Anyway, she's been living with Lenny, who's some drug-bitten, ass-hole guitarist friend of our Seamus, and has always seemed quite happy with the set-up. Wednesday night there's a pitiful knock at the front door round about twelve-thirty and it's Cary, along with a flood of tears and the biggest black eye I've ever seen. Turns out Lenny was busted by the pigs with some dope, thought it was all her fault, and beat her up. Anyroad, the poor chick's scared shitless, having got it into her head that all his 'gang' are after her too, so I said I'd put her up in the spare room so she could get on with her work in peace.

I know this smacks of over-protestation. I wouldn't have even bothered to tell you, but on Thursday morning Rick came round to drop off some crap he'd been reviewing for me, saw her flitting around in one of my dressing gowns, and all too obviously 'didn't like to say anything'. He must have said something, though, because like I say, the Lush was round like a shot that evening and didn't go until she'd finished your Glenfiddich (I had a bit too, to keep her company) and clapped eyes on Ms McNichol for herself. Now Cary isn't my type – far too young – but I won't lie, she is attractive. Probably very. And if I know Bingham like you know Bingham, she'll have written to you by the very next post.

PAY NO HEED

I guess that's all. Kinda hard writing to a brick wall, albeit a transcendental one. Write soon. Come home sooner – that weird phone call of yours awakened a dormant longing to feel your earlobes between my strong white teeth.

> I remain, ever faithful,
> Pluto. xxx

> Royal York Crescent
> Bristol 8
> Avon
> Very late Thursday night

Darling Mina,

This'll be short and sharp. I've tried to go to bed and not worry about this, which in my present condition would not be Sisyphean, but it's rankling, so I've got to speak to you, as it were. I'll give it to you straight.

I just dropped in on Randy, just to see how he was and so on, see if he had enough food etc. etc. and that McNichol girl walked in (don't know if you know her, but she's New York, twenty-one, absurdly lithe, and very, very pretty) and was all too palpably not popping in to drop off an essay. She wasn't exactly in one of his dressing gowns, but she came down from upstairs to say she was 'off to bed now' in a manner calculated to tell me it was time to leave, and she went upstairs again, into *your* bedroom.

There. I've told you. I had tried convincing myself that it was better for all concerned to pretend I didn't know, and to trust Randy to keep the whole thing well hidden, but that felt so bloody like late Henry James, treating you like the sacrificial angel figure you aren't and saying, 'Oh doesn't she take it too *beautifully*!' So, I've told you. Besides, what are friends for if not to tell you when your relationships need a little careful revision.

Please, Mina, don't think I'm telling you this out of aggression. Heaven knows I'm just not the type. If my hands weren't so full with keeping track of Rick's boyfriends and if I had more illusions about my personal charms, I might be after your man, but they are, I don't, so I'm not. Let's face it – I never could have kept a secret like that. I think it's better you hear now, when you've time and privacy to think things out, than later, when you might feel pressurized.

Darling Girl, if there's any way I can help, don't hesitate to let me know.

Love love love,
Ginny B. xxxxxxxx

18

The *Sunday Times* lay in pieces across her unmade bed. Domina was in her dressing gown. She sat at the typewriter, one leg tucked underneath her, sipping coffee and casting a critical eye over Saturday's work. Occasionally she would frown and, resting a page against the typewriter, make quick pencil revisions. It was only half-past nine, she had risen early to get to work. The hours before lunch were always the sharpest.

Saturday had seen the completed draft of a first act, a quick-paced playlet of ecclesiastical and maternal politics. Riding high on a sense of rekindled creative energy, she had worked almost all day. She had paused only to invite Des to tea by way of excusing herself from a film that evening, to assure Avril, fingers crossed, that she'd start work on the manuscript just as soon as she could polish off a friend's thesis on Job and Twentieth Century Suffering in Faith, and to buy a walnut cake. She had worked through until nearly midnight, when she had taken a congratulatory bath before accepting Thierry's invitation to come down to the kitchen and share some *boeuf en daube à la Provençale*, and fill in the conversational gaps left by Danny. Or was it Peter?

The three letters which Des had brought were now on the mantelpiece where they had been left after the third perusal. She had decided to consign the matter of the McNichol girl to cold storage where, though all was peaceful now, she suspected it would soon begin to make its presence felt.

Domina set aside the last, now corrected, page and fed a fresh piece of A4 into Ray, her faithful Olivetti.

'Act Two, Scene One,' she typed. 'A large bedsit in Shepherd's Bush. The room is freshly painted, yet irredeemably seedy – grotty furniture a must.' Then she stopped.

She stopped and stared at what she had typed. It was always the same – the exhaustive notes, the title, the stage directions, then the wait. The wait could last from ten minutes to ninety or more. She had learnt never to force herself. If nothing came and she sensed impending frustration, she would leave her typewriter and get on with something else. Occasionally the latter would be letter writing, more often it was related homework. She had no books on theological students or young priests, so she opted, after a longish wait and another cup of coffee, for letter writing.

'Dearest Pluto,' she wrote, then stopped. Someone had knocked at the door. 'Who is it?'

'Sorry. It's Quintus.' The door opened and the pale, decidedly interesting face appeared. 'Sorry. You're working, aren't you? I'll go away.'

'No. Do come in.' She slid a blank sheet over Saturday's work. 'It's only some typing.'

He was in a suit. It took her wholly by surprise. Something about him, perhaps the winceyette pyjamas, had led her to expect a dull, charcoal grey school affair. But this was lightweight wool, the Italian kind whose minute squares of black and white produce an almost silvery grey. It was faultlessly tailored, though from the slight overhang beyond each shoulder, she evinced for somebody else.

119

'What a lovely suit.'

'Oh.' He cast his eyes down and patted the material bashfully. 'It's ancient, really. It used to be my uncle's. We are almost the same size so it was handed down to me. Are you sure I'm not disturbing you?'

''Course not. Sit down.' He perched on an arm of the armchair. 'Are you going out?' she asked.

'Yes. I'm off to Eucharist.'

'Oh of course. Silly me.' Bloody fool.

'Actually, that's why I dropped in. Partly.'

'What?'

'Well, I wondered whether you'd like to come. To Santa Sofia. The music's special today.'

'Is it a Saint's day?'

'Sort of. Sorry. Of course you don't want to.'

'No.' She smiled. 'It would be rather fun. I've never seen an Orthodox service. But is it all right my coming? I'm not a member or anything.'

'As Philip said to Nathaniel, "Come and see".'

'But don't you have to bow and cross yourselves like mad? I won't have the first idea when to do things.'

He grinned. 'There aren't many points where you *have* to do anything. For the most part it's up to the individual. If you feel the need, you can lie flat on your face. There aren't any pews or seats, you see. We just stand in a crowd. You mustn't laugh – old biddies often leave half-way through to get on with Sunday lunch. It can be like Victoria Station.'

Domina sprang to her wardrobe.

'I must wear something black with sleeves – that much I do know.'

'Well, not if you . . .'

'It'll help me feel less conspicuous when I make howlers.'

'I'll be sitting on the porch. I've got to see Tilly to pay my rent.'

Apart from the brief revival of her faith after the success of *Onwards and Upwards* in the middle seventies, Domina had only set foot in church for funerals, weddings and for midnight mass, for which she reserved a nostalgic affection. As she walked with Quintus along Queensway to the Moscow Road, he explained things to the best of his ability, but failed to dispel her mounting sense of dread. She feared the inevitable sense of shame at her lapsed attendance and at being a voyeuse. As Quintus talked earnestly about the Diaspora, the Sacraments, the earthly heaven, the iconostasis and the Diakonikon, she trawled her mind for images of Greek Orthodoxy.

Apart from the obvious one of tall, bearded priests in high, black hats, she found only toothless, sabled crones who shut the windows in stifling Greek trains, solemn children in Corfu Town leading lambs on string, and a terrible, curiously guilt-ridden encounter with a cursing lavatory attendant in Knossos. Irreverently inappropriate snatches of *Fiddler on the Roof* would keep emerging as well, although she did her utmost to beat them back. Just as they were passing the bakery, she was saved by a sparkling recollection of a history lesson on the lawn in the convent cloisters. Sister Margaret was reading an extract from the *Russian Primary Chronicle*. It was brilliantly sunny and Domina had been paying her unwonted attention. The followers of Vladimir, a pagan prince of Kiev, arrived in

121

Constantinople at the end of their quest for the true religion. They found the Church of the Holy Wisdom and
were allowed to attend the Divine Liturgy.

'We knew not whether we were in heaven or on earth,'
read Sister Margaret who, though plain, was rumoured to
be charismatic. 'For surely there is no such splendour or
beauty anywhere upon earth. We cannot describe it to you:
only this we know, that God dwells there among men, and
that their service surpasses the worship of all other places.
For we cannot forget that beauty.' The memory gave Domina
succour; as ever, beauty should prove a point of access.

Quintus had said that visitors were welcome, but no one
seemed to notice her arrival.

'Do you want to go near the back?'

'Please,' she whispered back, 'it's beautiful.'

It wasn't terribly beautiful, in fact. The icons were
undoubtedly expensive reproductions, and the architecture
was similarly styled to type rather than to fancy. The most
disappointing thing was the congregation. Apart from the
few glaringly prominent converts and visitors, it was certainly composed of expatriate Greeks, but they were
expatriate to the point of drabness. There were a few who
had motored over from Knightsbridge and its environs,
and some well-heeled families from the Holland Park community, but the rest were indelibly Bayswater, with drawn
faces and characterless clothes. Domina's initial deflation
was acute.

Once the Proskomidia started, and she had overcome
her surprise at its being both in English and not so removed
from the common or garden Mass, she felt a gradual
change in the crowd before her. It was less that they became

more Greek than that they became more of a congregation. Her sense of exclusion swelled as that sense of unity of faith, of knowledge, of custom rose to the surface, and with that sense of exclusion came a perception of loveliness. The tonality of the hymns and chanting was alien, vaguely Slavonic, and unutterably sad. As the incense flowed, and was caught in the beams of light from the high windows, the icons seemed less blatantly new. As the first of the old women prostrated herself with a low Attic moan, the shades of Bayswater fled. The service had far more mystery, magic even, than any Roman Mass she had ever attended. She had witnessed pomp, certainly, as in High Mass at Saint Peter's, to which Mamma had so often taken her, and in the still dawn ceremonies in the little Lady Chapel at Saint Mary's she had felt herself in the presence of strong piety, but never had she felt such a powerful sense of conjury. It was partly a stage-managed effect, with music, smells, lights, gold and the eerie sound of Greek muttered defiantly in the face of the priest's English text. But there was something deeper than all this. Quintus had described the Orthodox belief that Eucharist is a joint celebration in which the congregation is as vital a participant as the priests, and it was this spirit of unanimous concentration, Domina reflected, that would have been extremely frightening were the service not taking place in the noonday sun.

When Quintus turned to whisper in her ear, she realized that she had not been following the service but had been staring, entranced at the activities before her.

'There's Brother Jerome, over there by the old man in the brown suit.'

She looked, found the old man in the brown suit, saw the man in a black cassock beside him, and was aghast. She turned her eyes at once to the front, so that Quintus should not see her concern. The similarity was undeniable, the suggestions, abhorrent. She glanced again to her left. As she did so, the man in the cassock turned to look at something to his right, and her fears were confirmed. It was Seb Saunders.

Seb Saunders had killed her cousin, or so it had always seemed to her. Seb was the presiding homosexual of her year. Everyone's year at Cambridge had one. Seb, who was one of those people who read philosophy because they already knew all there was to know about literature, had been hers. He was the only one who had ever posed a threat. He had been conspicuously beautiful, quite without the sickening taint of camp, and his notoriety lay in his ability to throw quite happily heterosexual men into confusion. Domina was not the only woman to have spent an exhausting night persuading her man that he was no less masculine for having been drawn into a dance, and at least tempted into more, with young Saunders. She had managed to keep Randy, but it was well known that many couples and even a marriage or two had been damaged by Seb's spell.

He had met Gregory at her twenty-first birthday party. Mamma and Jacoby had made one last, great effort, and had laid on a weekend in Sussex for her and as many of her friends as could be fitted on to a dance floor. The obligatory smattering of aunts and godparents had been there too, including her cousin. Six years her senior, Greg was an up-and-coming barrister. Amusing in her childhood, he had become necessarily conservative. At some stage in the party Seb had introduced himself, and the two of them were seen to spend the rest of the Saturday night side by side, deep in conversation. On the Sunday morning, amid the debris, they were perceived to have gone. Nothing extraordinary was read into this. Seb was a notorious party-leaver, and Gregory was known to be overladen with work in London. It was only the next term, when her cousin surprised her by paying frequent unexpected calls and was sighted on numerous occasions prowling Seb's college at night, that she realized he was besotted.

One morning Mamma appeared in Domina's rooms and announced that her quiet, rather pompous cousin had taken rat poison. Seb only slipped through his degree, having long since outgrown his syllabus, and was believed to have drifted to Greece and taken to small girls and ouzo. Nothing had been heard of him and he had entered the annals of brandy-fired reminiscence, a paradigm of burnt-out youthful folly.

Seeing Seb now, after so many years, Domina was ambushed by the pain of her cousin's death, a pain she had supposed to be quiescent. Seb had grown a beard.

'Oh God of spirits and of all flesh, who hast trampled down death and overthrown the Devil and given life unto Thy world: do Thou, the same Lord, give rest to the souls of Thy departed servants, in a place of light, refreshment, and repose, whence all pain, sorrow, and sighing have fled away. Pardon every transgression which they have committed, whether by word or deed or thought.'

As the prayer for the dead rose around her, Domina bit her lip in an effort not to cry, but felt the tears already brimming in her eyes. Her throat burnt. A sob came and she tried to turn it into a cough. Whipping out a handkerchief, she blew her nose and bit her knuckles through the linen. She was crying freely, out of love for Greg, concern for what might happen to Quintus, and terror lest Seb Saunders had recognized her. Turning, she hurried to the porch and found herself out on the steps in the sunshine whiteness. Standing for so long, and breathing the thick, scented air had made her dizzy. She allowed herself to sink into a crouching position on the steps.

'Domina, here. It's all right. What's the matter? I am sorry. I shouldn't have ... Was it the prayer for the Departed? Perhaps ... your husband?' Quintus was crouching beside her, beautifully suited, a long arm across her shoulders. She was mutely grateful for the proffered excuse.

'Oh. I'm so sorry.' She choked, and sounded her nose like a bugle. She mopped her eyes. 'Yes. It's so silly. It's well over a year, now. It does this. Just takes me by surprise. Normally I'm lucky and it happens when I'm alone, listening to the radio or something. Elgar.'

'Ssh. Don't talk. Here. Have mine. Yours is drenched.' He passed her a handkerchief. It was neatly ironed, white, with a blue Q in one corner.

'Thanks.' She blew her nose again and stood up. 'I am sorry. Look, I'll be OK. You go back inside.'

'Nonsense. I couldn't receive in any case.'

'Why ever not?'

'I haven't fasted.'

'Oh.'

'Let's walk around the block. It's nice and empty and you can talk.'

'Bless you.'

They set off in silence towards Leinster Square. The sun-splashed pavements were deserted. Here and there a radio could be heard clucking out Sunday morning requests. Nostalgia and roast beef hung in the air. Quintus seemed to be waiting for her to talk. Domina blew her nose hard on his handkerchief and stuffed it into her sleeve.

'I'll give it back when I've washed it,' she said.

'Oh. That's all right.'

'You know. My husband committed suicide.' He only frowned. She went on. 'I tell people it was galloping cancer, and it was in a way. He knew he had only a few weeks to live, and felt that it would make less suffering for me if he killed himself.'

'How awful. I . . .'

'It wasn't until then that I realized how little he could have known me. I'd have nursed him quite happily. Bedroom deaths are so kind. They give one time to come to terms with what is happening. Oh, I know it would have been painful for him, but the way he decided . . . It was the shock that was so cruel.'

'Do you want to . . . ?'

'Rat poison. We'd had rats, you see, so there were tins of the stuff in the potting shed. I think it contains some form of cyanide. You add water and it produces a poisonous gas.' Domina could feel the conversation twisting away from her grasp, yet the game of his discomfiture was intoxicating. 'Do you believe it's a sin – suicide?'

'Well, I . . . I've always thought it depended on the circumstances. Despair is a sin, because it implies insuperable doubt, but one could do it out of mercy, and that certainly isn't a sin. Sometimes I think it would be good to die for joy, in a sort of extremity of worship. I mentioned that to Brother Jerome as it worried me, and he said that an element of selfish joy could always be perceived in martyrdom but only from a doubting viewpoint – if one couldn't understand that the pleasure of worship is selfless.'

'Why wasn't Brother Jerome up at the altar, behind the . . . er . . . the—?'

'The iconostasis?'

'Yes.'

'Because he isn't a priest. He's just a monk. Well, I say "just", but actually it means much more in some ways. The monks and the priests function side by side. The priests have a responsibility to their flock and parish and lead the congregation in the celebration of the Eucharist, but they tend not to go any higher in the hierarchy. In Greece they're usually married villagers. The monks take vows of celibacy and abstinence, and can progress to become hierodeacons, and bishops and so forth.'

'Oh. I see. So he's simply attached to the parish as a kind of theologian-in-residence.'

'In a way. I think he should be a priest because he's a good speaker, but he never really talks about himself.'

'Just about you.'

'Well, me if I bring the subject up, otherwise just the Bible and the ways of the Church.'

'How did you meet him?'

'He came up to me, after I'd been to my first service there. I was trying to read the notices on the board outside, but they're mostly in Greek, and he came up to ask if he could help.'

'I see.' They continued for a while without speaking, and turned back into Princes Square.

'What were you working at this morning?' he asked suddenly.

'Just some typing. Dear mad Avril's given me some top secret manuscript to type out for her, and I've got a friend's thesis to do. It's deadly dull, but I find I can do it and think of something else at the same time.'

'Will you want to get back to that this afternoon?'

'Why do you ask?' She turned and was startled by a sweet expectancy on his face. He laughed. 'Why?' she asked again.

'I wondered whether you'd like to come flying. I'm booked in for an outing this afternoon. It's an old Chipmunk of my father's. He keeps it there free of charge in return for allowing the instructors to use it. His eyesight's not good enough any more, you see. I can go up whenever I like, so long as I book in advance. Would you like to?'

'Oh, that'd be marvellous! Are you sure I won't be in the way? There must be so many friends clamouring to be taken. What about Penny or someone?'

'No. Honestly. I'd much rather take you.' Embarrassed by the intensity of her smile he looked ahead again. 'Cheer you up,' he mumbled.

As they hurried back to Inverness Terrace to change, Domina wanted to whistle.

c/o Dr D.B. Turner
Top Floor
37a Gloucester Road
London SW7
Sunday evening

Darling Pluto,

Thank you for your enchanting letters. I've been writing to you in my head for days, and keep thinking I've put pen to paper when in fact you're still aching to hear from me. It's late and I'm sitting in the mystery garret with a carton of pineapple juice. It's unbelievably humid. Someone in a room near me is playing Louis Armstrong (Saint James Infirmary??) and I miss you badly. Hi there.

Oh Rand, I'm having such *fun*. I'm dying to tell you all. It's a houseful of faggots, morticians, tarts and Trappist monks – well, practically. I don't know about finding myself, but I'm certainly collecting tomes of material . . .

I did laugh. Of course Bingham wrote by the very next post, and of course I'm totally untouched by her insinuations. That woman gives good neighbours a bad name. As if I'd leave you alone for a day if I had the slightest fears about you sleeping around your department! God

knows, laying nubile undergrads because your time is
running out is hardly in your inimitable style. (Who *is*
this McNichol brat anyway?) The Lush probably just fan-
cies one of her new ASMs and is working out her guilty
aggression. Good boy to tell me though; her letter would
have been a nasty shock read cold.

Oh Christ, now they're playing Billie Holiday – one of
the *really* depressing ones. I think I must go to bed
before I develop a 'negative attitude'. This scribble is
artless but comes with keen and tender love from

Minnie Mouse. xxxx

PS Remember one Seb Saunders? Have I found out an
interesting development about *him* . . .

The Paragon

Clifton

Bristol 8

Avon

Saturday morning

Domina,

You're going to be mad at reading this, so get into a
large open space before going any further.

Oh shit. I don't know how to get this down. Look. I'll
be short, because apologies would be irritating and
futile, and I believe we understand one another enough
for them to be unnecessary over something like this.

I've slept with Cary McNichol. Classic hopeless male
thing to say, I know, but I really didn't want to or mean
to. I swear nothing had happened when I wrote to you

yesterday morning. I really did just want to stop Ginny throwing the shit at the fan like that. I'd been sleeping in the study on the camp bed, and she'd been sleeping upstairs, in the spare room. Anyway, the long and the short of it is that I got a bit stoned last night and started feeling blue and apologetic, as is my merry wont, and suddenly I just had to sleep in our bed and hug your teddy or something. So I went up and clambered in and, Oh God, she was there and one thing led inexorably to another.

It's now the morning after the night before that I hadn't meant to happen. I woke up feeling like something out of the nastier corners of the Old Testament. Cary has vanished without trace and I can't say I blame her. I feel guilty and if she was around I'd want to give her another black eye. Dammit, I can't even remember if it was any good. I don't even fancy her.

I'm writing to you straight away – I guess out of the purely selfish motive of allaying a sore conscience. I think I've a pretty good idea of how you'll react, and I deserve whatever you intend to throw at me. The next move is most certainly your own. All I'll do is say, 'This happened, but I love you and don't want to lose you. Never.'

Shamefaced.
Randolph.xxx

20

It was Monday afternoon.

'Please, could you tell me where I can find theology reference books?'

'Upstairs,' Domina was told by the girl inside the bleeping check-out machine. 'You go through that arch, then up the stairs to the second floor. When you come in there's a reception desk straight ahead of you. Turn right and it's the first bay of shelves on your left, by the philosophy books.'

'Thank you.'

Domina pushed through the turnstile and followed the directions. A large watercolour hung over the first landing. It was called 'All Generations Shall Call Me Blessed' and showed the Virgin in garish majesty, surrounded by various saints and important figures, historical and Kensington. Beneath the heavy frame there dangled a key to the work, with each figure in silhouette linked by a number to a name on a long list. She pushed through the swing doors, turned right and found the first bay on the left. It was empty of readers. She slung her shoulder bag onto the desk. Randy's letter slid out and on to the floor. She picked it up and stuffed it inside.

She had posted her bland little missive on Sunday night before going to bed, and had picked his up in the hall on her way out this morning. It said 'urgent' on the envelope, so Des must have driven over and dropped it off. There was a message on the back.

'Just can't keep our good thing at bay, can we? Urgent my arse. Give me a ring sometime. Hope all's productive. Des.' Letters that passed each other in the mail were matched for irritation value only by telephones unintentionally off the hook and broken egg yolk in meringue mixture. She had read his news three times as she walked down Kensington Church Street to the library, and her heart had not missed a beat. This could have been a symptom of delayed rage, but she doubted it.

On Sunday night she had written the first scene of Act Two, introducing the youngish Fay to the much younger Barnaby. The unaccustomed conversion of life into comedy didn't feel like cheating. She had always supposed it would.

As they had driven through London in his battered Morris 1000 he had asked her to call him Quin. The weather at Biggin Hill had been astonishing. The air was still, the sky cloudless, and she had felt the heat radiating off the tarmac onto her bare legs as they crossed the airfield. She had never flown in a light aircraft before, had travelled in nothing smaller than great, fat Boeings to the Mediterranean and America. Large aeroplanes only scared her as they hurtled along the runway. As Quin talked shop to the technician who was doing something to the engine, she wondered whether she was going to be afraid.

'Quin, I've never been up in one of these before. Will it be rough?'

'It's wonderful!'

'But is it rough?'

'Depends on the weather. There's absolutely no wind down here. There could be some nasty currents higher up. We'll have to see. Domina, you look terrified.'

'No. I'm not really. Just excited.'

'Look, you sit in that seat back there. It's always a bit nerve-racking sitting right at the front as we take off. Then, once we're up, you can come forward and sit by me when you're ready.'

'You are sweet.'

'All right? Belt fastened?'

'Chocks away.'

She sat, strapped in, and played with her fingers as he made the final preparations and they began to coast over what seemed an excessively bumpy runway. The noise was deafening at first, and everything around her seemed to be shaking itself loose. She broke out in a sweat. Then, quite suddenly the shaking stopped, the noise dropped, and she felt her stomach swing away below her. She laughed.

'Are we up? I daren't look.'

'Yes. Isn't it great?'

'I still daren't look.'

'Don't be silly. We're quite safe. Even if the engine fell off, we're so light we'd fairly glide down. Go on. Have a look.'

Domina raised her eyes and found the plane ablaze with light and the fields spread out far below her. The aerodrome resembled a toy garage.

'Oooh! God!'

'Are you going to be sick?'

'No. I'm just getting used to it. Quin, you are clever. How old were you when you first came up?'

'Eighteen – that was the first time on my own – well, with Pa sitting in the seat beside me.'

'Is he very proud of you?'

'Come and sit up here so you can see properly. I'll keep her straight so you don't fall flat.'

She unfastened her belt and lurched forward to the front passenger seat where she hurriedly strapped herself in again.

'How long can we stay up for?'

'Not too long because Brian wants her for a lesson. We were a bit slow driving here.'

For a while they had flown in near silence. Quintus concentrated on the controls while Domina found herself keeping up a running commentary on what she could see. It was after about a quarter of an hour that he frightened her. At the time, the wild idea suggested itself that he had befriended her, wooed her almost, simply to be able to take her up to a great height then scare the wits out of her. In retrospect she saw that it was nothing so shallow. He was evidently a very still water.

It began when he had taken them suddenly higher, in a great swoop that drew Domina's breath away. She laughed nervously, then turned away from the window to see his face transfigured. His eyes were quite off the dials and controls, staring out into the thin blue beyond them, and a smile darted through his lips as he spoke.

'It's funny, but when I'm up this high it feels like . . . well . . . the closest you can get to God without dying.' His joy held her dumb. 'It's like the Icarus painting,' he continued, 'we're so fragile up here. I could just cut the engines and let us glide slowly into that wood.'

Domina remembered a snatch of Middle English and threw it at him,

' "A feather on the breath of God"? Do you think it's true people fall asleep before they hit the ground?'

'I wouldn't be surprised. I think if you wanted to die that way, you'd certainly fall quietly. There would come a point where you reached maximum velocity and it would be quite peaceful.'

'I think I should panic. Imagine if you changed your mind when it was too late.'

'It's never too late. Not in a plane. You can pull them out of a dive surprisingly late, just as long as you keep calm. Do you want to glide?'

'What?'

'Look. I'll show you. It's wonderful. It's like in *The Protevangelium of James*.'

'The *what*?' The boy was mad or drunk.

'*The Protevangelium of James*, where time stands still for the birth of Christ.'

He leant over and deftly flicked a switch. There was a stuttering and then silence. The engine had stopped.

'Oh my God . . .' Domina started, then realized that there was no sickening drop.

They were gliding onwards in silence.

'See?' Quin turned and his smile was almost gleeful.

' "A feather on the breath of God",' Domina muttered. Then she caught an image of a balsa wood glider, the kind she had made from half-crown kits as a child, sailing in a gentle arc upwards, then coming to a sudden halt in its rise before taking a nose dive. Any minute now the trees were going to come roaring up towards them. 'For Christ's sake,

Quintus, don't be a little fool. Start the fucking engine or you'll kill us both!'

Even as her anger flared up and he swiftly obeyed, she sensed her expletive jar crudely with the scene he had begun to create. The engine coughed back into life and at once she felt as though he had made a pass and she had given him a cruel rebuffal.

'Oh Quin, I'm so sorry. I didn't . . .'

'No. Honestly. It was all my . . .'

'No. I just suddenly felt so scared. I thought we were going to die.'

'I should have warned you. It was unfair to take you by surprise like that. We must go down now.'

'Must we?'

'Time for Brian to take her over.'

On the journey home their stilted conversation had petered out swiftly. He had the radio tuned in to Radio Three. The aggressive classicism alienated her and she had fallen to staring at the side of the road. Back in the house he had saved the situation with the gesture of making tea, and she had been able to make cheerful conversation through two cups before sloping off to Act Two.

'Sorry. I wonder if you could help me?'

'We do our best. What seems to be the problem?'

The man behind the desk was insufferable, as Quin had warned her.

'Well, I'm trying to find a copy of *The Protevangelium of James*. I've looked all through the theology section but, well, to be quite frank, I'm not sure I know what I'm looking for.'

His patronage enraged her. 'Is it a work of theology,' he asked, 'or a piece of theological fiction?'

'I think it's some kind of sacred text.'

'Let's see.' He began to slide a microfiche through a viewing machine. 'Prob ... Prog ... Prom. It really does help if you can find out who publishes the thing, you know.'

'Hello, Domina. What's the problem?' It was Avril, string bag in hand.

'Hello. You haven't heard of *The Protevangelium of James*, have you?'

'Of course. It'll be over here in Theology. It's a non-canonical gospel.' She inclined her head at a confidential angle. 'My little man seems to know the thing backwards. Fairly obscure, but it seems to have a strong oral-traditional background.'

Domina turned back to the desk where the man was looking piqued.

'Thank you so much,' she said.

'There we are, my dear. *The Non-Canonical Gospel Texts*. Nineteen fifty-three, but I don't imagine much has changed since then.'

'Thanks, Avril.'

'How goes the typing?'

'Oh. Well. I'm starting on yours this afternoon.'

'Probably take you an age to decipher my arachnid scrawl. Take your time, though, take your time. Glad I could be of some help.' So whispering, she headed for the sociology table.

Domina sat and began to read. Mary's childhood in the temple was described, and the singling out of Joseph to be the saintly guardian. She read fast, skipping over much of the text, then was pulled up short by chapter eighteen:

18.2. Now I, Joseph, was walking, and yet I did not walk, and I looked up to the air and saw the air in amazement. And I looked up at the vault of heaven, and I saw it standing still and the birds of the heaven motionless. And I looked at the earth, and saw a dish placed there and workmen lying round it, with their hands in the dish. But those who chewed did not chew, and those who lifted up anything lifted up nothing, and those who put something to their mouth put nothing to their mouth, but all had their faces turned upwards.

21

The night had been sticky and troubled and now someone was trying to batter down her door. She was unable to write on her return from the library and had seized on the opportunity of going to bed as a diversion and escape. She could not sleep, however. The air was tight with mustering storm, the bedding seemed dotted with biscuit crumbs, and a family nearby were broadcasting a film of the action-packed variety. She lay listening to the succession of explosions and screaming women for a while, wondering whether it was one she had seen, then was driven out of bed by the intimate wail of a mosquito. Cursing, she had pulled on a frock and some sandals and decided on a walk around the block. Tilly was sitting out on the porch, so she had stayed to talk to her instead. Rather, Tilly talked and Domina listened, too tired to contribute much. They watched the laughing boys and stealthier elders passing in and out of the Hermes Club. They held a brief exchange with Thierry and Nick (or was it Alan?), as they came in, then she had tried to sleep once more. She lay awake for perhaps another half an hour, resisting the temptation to call on Quin when she heard him return from a vigil, before falling prey to a night of sickly erotic dreams involving a quantity of sleek machinery and miscellaneous liturgical symbols. She had woken, quite unrefreshed, to a thick, grey sky above which the sun was evidently scorching.

The batterer-down of the door was Mrs Moorhouse with an announcement that Westminster Bureau had telephoned, that she, Mrs Moorhouse, had failed to wake her, that they asked her urgently to ring back when she woke, and that they had telephoned several times the day before when she was out. This news took a deadening effect on what was already a spiritless awakening. Domina swung her feet onto the nylon carpet and felt a gnawing ache in her lumbar vertebrae. Old Faithful. Her period was under five days away. Any attempt at creativity would be futile. Last time she had been in Tuscany, the backache had come on and Aunt Juliana-Costanza had explained that it was the BVM's way of reminding women of their duty to bear children.

'She send you the ache at your most fruitful time, *cara*. It is to remind you of the sweet pang of maternal labour. Your dear Mamma, she used to have that pain, just like you, then you were born and it went away! Marry your Randolph, have a *bambino*, and Holy Mary will take away this little pain.'

Consigning Santa Maria di Dappertutto, Juliana-Costanza, helpful nuns and all other wise virgins to the Pit, Domina scowled her way to the kitchen in search of coffee. There, Thierry bewailed the fact that he was doomed to be used and discarded like a how-you-say man-size tissue and she snapped at him. On the way back to her room she hid with her breakfast in a bathroom, having seen Avril coming, whistling, from above, felt immediate guilt and found a task to see her through till lunch-time.

She was surprised to find that Avril's manuscript was highly entertaining. The English was not the most stylish animal, but she patted that into shape here and there as she typed. The substance of the tale, even though she had, or perhaps because she had made so much of it up, was extraordinary. The discrepancy between La Gilchrist's tone and the unparalleled sleaziness of her subject matter was unwittingly amusing – as if Louisa May Alcott had paraphrased the symposia of de Sade. By half-past twelve Domina had typed as far as Avril had written, up to Padraic's discovery and first, not so tentative, explorations of his carnal tastes. By twenty-five to one she had decided that a photocopy of the work so far must be handed to Des for professional perusal. Flared by the thought that she might have stumbled on a bestseller *malgré-lui*, Domina was embarking on a letter to Virginia to thank her for her letters, quash her conjectures, and demand that she write to a certain Penelope Havers in Bayswater offering her an audition, when she heard voices on the landing.

'Did it say which number his room was, downstairs?'

'No. Just how many times to ring his bell.'

'Why he insisted on living here I can't imagine.'

'Well, you know Quin.'

'That's a pointless observation.'

'Well, don't . . .'

Domina's curiosity beguiled her caution and she opened the door.

'Hello,' she said.

They were a man and a woman. He six foot five and almost bald, she much shorter, with brassy, back-combed hair. She was aggressively well-preserved, but Domina guessed that each verged on fifty.

'Good morning,' said the man.

'Hello. We're looking for Quintus Harding,' said she, loudly and distinctly, as to a backward child.

Quintus was chez 'Brother Jerome'. She had seen his back view leaving by the front door. He had been carrying some books.

'Quin's out, I'm afraid. I saw him leave about two hours ago.'

'Oh dear,' said the man.

The woman was giving Domina a thorough inspection, her teeth half bared in a smile for strangers.

'Was he expecting you?' asked Domina.

'Well, rather,' said the woman. 'We'd arranged to take him out to lunch.' Her voice was clipped by a system of Forces intonation that just failed to mask the occasional slurring of a consonant. 'Do you . . . er . . . know Quintus, then?'

'Well, slightly. I only moved in last week, but sharing a landing we tend to bump into one another. Sorry, I'm Domina Tey. How d'you do?'

'How d'you do?'

'Hello again.' She shook hands with each.

'We're his parents,' added Mr Harding.

'I'm sure she's guessed that already.' Mrs Harding threw Domina a glance that dared her not to smile in complicity. Domina smiled briefly back and wished she had stayed in her room. 'So this is his room?' Mrs Harding gave a firm shove on her son's door. 'Locked,' she noted. 'Don't suppose you've any idea when he'll be back?' Mr Harding was engrossed in the instructions on the landing fire extinguisher.

'I'm afraid not.'

'Two hours ago he went, you say?'

'Yes.'

'Well, he's normally terribly punctual.'

Domina saw there was no alternative but to invite them into her room to wait.

'Would you like to wait in my room till he gets back?' she offered.

'Wouldn't that be a bore? Don't you have to be at work or something?'

'I work from home, actually.'

'Well, thank you very much.' Mrs Harding followed Domina into the room. She let the door swing shut with a bang while Domina hurriedly snatched a bra out of the armchair and stuffed it under her pillow.

'Do sit down.'

Mrs Harding sat in the chair, Domina on the bed. Mr Harding knocked on the door.

'Come in.'

'No need to knock, you fool,' his wife called out. 'Actually we're here to tell Quin about our divorce.'

'Oh.'

'Look there's no need . . .'

'Oh, don't be a child, Hamish. Everyone's getting them now.' Hamish was hovering misplaced, about a chair full of books. 'I'm sure Miss . . . er?'

'Mrs Tey.'

'I'm sure Mrs Tey knows lots of separated couples.'

'My parents, as a matter of fact,' said Domina. 'Let me put those on the floor for you.' She cleared the hard-backed chair for Hamish, who perched on it as though used to breaking things. She wondered how they had ever managed in bed, then decided that it must have been separates from day one.

'Really?' asked Mrs. 'And how old were you?'

'Twenty-two. I'd just finished at Cambridge.'

'A Cambridge girl, eh?' asked Hamish.

'Yes. That's right.'

'Well anyway, we've come to break the tidings to Quintus. I think he's known for ages. Actually, I'm a bit nervy.'

'Why?'

'About telling him. He's frightfully pi, you know.'

'Oh.'

Domina was acutely embarrassed. It was a conversation she wanted to push much further, simply because his parents were so improbable, so explanatory – but the aggression condoned in allowing Mrs Harding to continue was ugly. The topic seemed to have been dropped now. Hamish was reading the back of one of the novels from the library. Mrs, who contrived to make a linen suit and court shoes smart to the point of militarism, was sliding interestingly off balance. Domina wondered whether the situation was strange to her, whether Quintus had had few friends for her to meet.

'Have you lived here long?' his mother asked, then sensed her blunder and ran a hand over her powdered forehead. 'Oh no. Of course, last week. You said. So you work from here?'

'That's right. Normally I'm a school teacher, but I'm typing manuscripts at the moment while I look for a new job.'

'What age group do you teach?'

'Under thirteens, mostly. I used to teach up at Durham.'

'Durham, eh?' asked Hamish, crossing his extensive legs the other way, and selecting another book.

'Yes,' said Domina. 'Do you know it well?'

'He was stationed about thirty miles away for about a month, I expect. It's pointless asking him questions like that. No memory for places at all.'

'Oh. Oh dear.'

There was a pause. Mrs Harding opened her handbag and took out a handkerchief. Domina noted with satisfaction that it bore lipstick stains. The nose was blown. Domina smoothed her pillow. The handkerchief returned to the bag which clicked shut. Mrs Harding looked up and for a moment stared Domina full in the face. Then she broke into another smile for strangers and said, 'The worst thing about coming to visit one's children is that there's never any Scotch.' As she spoke, the door opened and Quintus came in. 'Darling.'

'Mother, hello.' They kissed. 'Father.' They shook hands.

'Kind Mrs Tey has been entertaining us while we waited for you.'

'Oh no . . . I mean, have you been waiting long? I came back as quickly as I could.'

'No. Not long.' Both parents were now standing. Domina had forgotten quite how tall Hamish was.

'Now, I want to see inside your room,' said Mrs Harding.

'It's terribly messy. You can see it after lunch. We'll miss our table otherwise. Where's the car?'

'On a meter. Your father actually managed to find one.'

'You start on down and I'll catch you up.'

'All right. So nice to have met you,' she said, and gave Domina a cold, dry hand.

'Yes,' added Hamish, and proffered her a vast one.

Quintus herded them out onto the stairs, then darted back into Domina's room.

'I say, I am sorry.'

'Not at all. It was lovely to meet them.'

'I'd completely forgotten they were coming. Were they here for ages?'

'No. No. You rush off and join them.'

'Thanks.'

'Have a nice lunch,' she said as he went, then remembered that they were here to tell him about the divorce. She remained on the edge of the bed, listening to him unlock his door and set his books on his table. She heard the door close, and his feet scurrying down the stairs two at a time. He was lucky not to be as tall as his father.

Her mind only half on the task in hand, Domina finished the letter to Virginia and set out to post it. As she turned from locking her door, she saw that Quin had left the keys in his. She stood for a moment, looking down into the stairwell and along the narrow corridor that led to the lavatory and bathroom. All was silent. She let herself into the room, taking the key with her, and shut the door.

The Brueghel poster had been pinned to the wall. With no sun to stream in over the geranium, it made the room feel darker. She wasn't sure what she wanted to see. There was a shirt, the one he had worn the day before, tossed to the floor in one corner. She snatched it up and plunged her face into it. The pale blue cotton was cool on her skin. She realized as she breathed in through it that Quintus had a familiar scent

148

about him, familiar because she always relished it when loading Seamus' things into the washing machine. The closest analogy was grilled bacon. A young actor in Ginny's company had it too. It made her want to growl.

She cast aside the shirt and crouched to the record-player. Bach's third cello suite. Certain that this was the one, she put it on. She was right. She turned her eyes to the table, and his books. *The Way of the Ascetics, Living Prayer, The Festal Menaion, Lenten Triodion.* She could not imagine the boy, the attractive young man, actually sitting down here and reading such things. The idea was faintly disgusting. More repellent was the image of him closeted with the *soi-disant* Brother Jerome to discuss them. Beside the books lay a spiral-bound notebook. 'Quintus Harding' was carefully inscribed in the top right-hand corner. She opened it and read at random:

7th, 11th and 12th Articles define a system of Eschatology. Double judgement, one at the hour of death – not final, the other, Final, at the end of time. First judgement can be alleviated by prayers of the faithful.

Vincent of Lerins: *quod semper quod ubique ad omnibus (formula).* Ergo, highest authority are the 7 Ecumenical councils from everywhere (*Ubique*) only established formulae for what had always been said (*Semper*).

She flicked over some more pages.

In 1913 there were officially 32 diocese, 4025 parishes, 6 Archbishops, 25 Bishops, 167 monasteries, 10 convents and approx. 1,922,000 souls.

She shut the notebook in disgust, turning it over as she did so, to see:

> For details of seminary try:—
> Holy Cross Seminary Press
> 79 Goddard Avenue
> Brookline
> Massachusetts 02186

Could he be serious? Could anyone be so *very* serious?

With a sigh, Domina sat on the end of his bed. She picked up the record box that lay there beside her and stared blankly at Casals' egg of a head. The photograph had been tinted blue which lent him an extraterrestrial air. She dropped the box to the floor. The bed was unmade. Unlikely that, nearly suspicious. She reached out a hand and ran it over the rumpled lower sheet. The bedding was cheerful, Habitat stuff. A sensuality bolted down. She rolled to one side and stretched out, face downwards on his bed, sniffing deep the bacon smell off his duvet, his sheets, his pillow. There were a few bloodstains on the pillow, from a nosebleed, perhaps. The music was reaching the point that always sent Randy into the yelps of raw delight that he reserved for music, food and sex. They drew attention to the womanly fullness of his lips. Thinking of Randy, she raised her eyes from the pillow. There was a little bookshelf-cum-bedside table to her left. On the hidden, pillow side, a square of card had been stuck to the side of a box of tissues:

> How great was the purity and sanctity of him who was chosen the guardian of the most spotless Virgin (Butler's *Lives*).

She laughed aloud, but shock knocked her silent. There was a copy of *Sinful Living* on the shelf. Frowning, she sat up and pulled it out. The French's edition. She looked inside the cover. 'Quintus Harding, Bayswater' it said, and the date of the day before yesterday. Quickly, Domina pushed the book back onto the shelf and tugged out a dusky pink document file that had lain beneath it. She opened it and found photocopies. They were photocopies of reviews of her plays. There were four photographs of her, taken with a polaroid: two of her in the street, taken through the area railings, one of her in the Gardens sitting on a bench and one of her back view climbing the stairs. There were two pages cut out of last November's *Plays and Players* with photographs of her and an interview, and there, stuffed in the corner of the file, were the laddered tights she had thrown out two mornings ago.

Domina sat through the second movement of the Suite, looking from clipping to clipping, over to the desk, up at the icon of Joseph, then back to the things in the file. Her immediate reaction was one of bewildered hilarity, that an embryo saint should be obsessed with her. She pictured his tortured guilt as he took a razor blade to the library copies of *Plays and Players*, smirked at his discomfort were he caught with the tights in his hot little hand. Then she reflected that Quintus's hands weren't hot, that he was a restrained, cool person, and that he had, with restraint, coldness indeed, been deceiving her since they met. He had played along with the deceptions that now seemed so pathetic in one of her age. He had been humouring her and doubtless Seb was in on the joke. Seb Saunders might even have instigated the joke. Here was silly old Domina Tecum, spoiling for one last fling, and his young bit could prove the perfect means to her humiliation. At best, Seb knew nothing, and she was providing a young fan with the peculiar experience of a lifetime. At worst, they chuckled over her together.

A lump rose to her throat. She took some deep breaths to dissolve it. A single tear spilled down her cheek, and she drew an iron calm about her. She stuffed the clippings, the photographs, the tights, back into the folder and returned it to the bedside shelf. She turned off the record-player, picked up the letter for Virginia and left, leaving the key in the door. She had to buy wine, cheese, bread, perhaps some chocolates and nuts, and she must take a long, long bath. There was no hurry. She scribbled an invitation on a scrap of paper she found in the hall and left it folded in his slot of the letter rack. She ran her fingers through her hair, shook out her skirt, and let herself out. She would eat a late, slow lunch with Des; they could discuss Avril's manuscript.

22

She was in the bath when he returned. It was quite late in the evening. Either lunch had extended into dinner, or the parental bombshell had sent him reeling to Seb for aid. She turned off the hot tap with a big toe and listened. He went into his room, then came out and knocked on her door. There was a pause during which she guessed he pushed open the door to look inside. He called her name softly, then returned to his room. Soon she heard loud choral music coming along the landing. It might have been the Saint Matthew Passion, but she couldn't be sure. She wondered if he was weeping below the voices. She tugged out the plug with her foot, stood, and wrapped her towel about her. Back in her room she dressed in the clothes she had selected; nothing wild, but nothing remotely C of E. She slid a new jazz cassette into the tape section of her radio and, humming gently, lit some candles and dabbed some Métale behind each ear. She brought the wine out of the sink where it had been breathing in some warm water, and set it on the floor along with the plates, cheese, grapes and walnuts. She pushed the chocolates under the bed with her foot: chocolate was the replacement, not the aperitif. She made one last pout in the looking glass, pushing back her hair, then crossed the landing.

'Quin?'

She knocked and pushed the door open. He was lying

on his bed staring up at the ceiling. She guessed he had been trying to cry and had failed. The record had finished. He sat up abruptly.

'Domina, hello.'

'Did you get my note?'

'No?'

'Oh. I left you a note in the letter rack asking you to supper – well, to share a bottle of wine.'

'Oh, yes please. That would be lovely.' He stood, and switched off the record-player.

'Is everything all right?'

'Yes. No. Well . . .'

'I'm afraid your mother told me why they were here.'

They walked through the gloom into her room. She slipped the catch on the lock as he passed by her and sat on the floor against the bed.

'It looks nice,' he said, 'with the candles.'

'I found the sticks in the kitchen cupboards when I was looking for nutcrackers.'

She sat across the floor from him, her back against the armchair. She poured two glasses of wine.

'Thank you,' he said and, toasting her mutely, raised a glass to his lips. Domina drank also. It was a good Bordeaux, but she should have opened it earlier.

'How do you feel about them,' she asked, 'about your parents?'

He ate a walnut, staring into the nearest candle. 'It disgusts me,' he said.

She could not hide her dismay. 'What?' she exclaimed.

'They're too old, and they should know better.'

'But if they're unhappy, then surely . . .' This priggishness would make her task a great deal easier.

'I mean that they're too old to start afresh; they'll only be lonely. Besides, marriage is a Sacrament.'

'You don't honestly believe that?'

'Yes. Of course I do.' His voice was matter-of-fact. The way he raised his eyes to hers as he spoke confirmed the plainness of his faith.

'Sorry. I'm not mocking or anything,' she assured him, refilling his glass, 'it's just that my parents separated when I was about your age, and all I could think was how happy they were going to be. I only wondered why they hadn't split up before.'

'Why hadn't they?'

'They were "protecting" me.'

'You say "separated", did they actually get a divorce?'

'No. Mamma's too devout.'

'She believes marriage is a Sacrament?'

'Certainly.'

'But you didn't laugh at her?'

'Of course I laughed. I laugh about it whenever we meet, because there were so many dishy men lining up to run off with her, and I know she wanted to run but was fooling herself that her duty lay with my father.'

'What did your husband make of your attitudes?'

She refilled her glass and topped up his. It was vital that he drink more swiftly than her; she must do all the talking.

'Oh, cut the crap, Quin. You know I've never had a husband.'

'What?'

'Look. You left the key in your bedroom door and I let myself in and nosed around and found that file by your bed.'

His face blanched, then reddened. His eyes flicked away from her. She was certain he was about to spill the wine.

'Oh dear,' he said.

'Since you knew who I was, why did you string me along like that?'

'I . . . I suppose I rather liked the person you were being.' He looked up with one of his crushed-in smiles and she had to throw back her head and laugh.

'Oh Christ!' she declared. 'I'm a silly fool, and you're so sweet.'

She cut herself a slice of Bleu de Bresse and discovered that she was getting drunk. She should never have had that strengthening gin before her bath. She chewed on the cheese, picked off some grapes and listened to the crooning blues number that was playing.

'So how does it feel to be eating in the bedsit of a prize-winning playwright?'

'I'm honoured. I've seen every one of your plays, you know.'

She laughed. 'You haven't! Really? But they're tripe.'

'No they're not. They aren't pretentious, that's all. They're humane and they make me laugh.'

'And they're tripe.'

'What *are* you doing here?'

'It's a secret.' She cut off a piece of Brie and refilled his glass. 'No. Actually, I've just split up with my boyfriend. We'd been living together for years now, married in all but name, and I thought I'd move in here while I found myself somewhere new to live.'

'You liked it for its anonymity?'

'Huh. Yes. That's right.' The boy had a sense of irony after all. She didn't want him to ask about the new play, so she swung the subject around. 'Quin?'

'Yes?'

'Do you really believe what you said about your parents' divorce?'

'Yes.'

'Aren't you – forgive me if I sound patronizing – aren't you a trifle young to be so dogmatic?'

'I don't think so. Dogma's only an outsider's word for faith.'

'Did Brother Jerome tell you that?'

'Yes. But that doesn't make it any less true.'

'You know his name isn't really Jerome?'

'Of course. It used to be Sebastian, but he changed it when he took his vows. People often change their names to strengthen their sense of starting afresh.'

'Do you mind me cross-examining you like this?'

'Fire away, only child.'

'What do you want to do when you leave UCL?'

'I've applied to go to the Holy Cross Seminary in Massachusetts. It was a choice of there or Athens, and I'm hopeless at learning languages.'

'So you really want to be a priest?'

'Well, I want to be a monk, then see what happens. I don't think I'd be terribly good at pastoral work – I'm not very good at understanding people's problems. As you would say, I'm "dogmatic". I went to see Jerome after lunch today. I'd barely got back from there when you knocked on my door.'

'Did you talk to him about your parents?'

'No. Not much, anyway. But having talked to them has helped me make up my mind. I'm taking my first vows next week.'

'Which? Monastic ones?'

'Sort of. Strictly speaking I'm not meant to until I'm several years older, so these would be unofficial, preliminary ones. They'll be just as binding, of course; a sort of personal preparation for me.'

'On approval,' said Domina with bitterness.

'Quite.'

'Quintus, don't you think it's a terrible waste?' She saw him hesitate. His delay could not be mistaken. The boy was a suicidal idiot.

'I don't see why. I've no other ambitions. I've no particular skills. I like history, and as a monk I could still study. My faith is the most exciting thing that's ever happened to me.'

'Better than flying?'

'Oh that. I'd give that up.'

'Why? You enjoy it.'

'I couldn't afford it, for one thing.'

'And you wouldn't mind that?'

'Of course I'd mind at first, but that's irrelevant.'

She poured him another glass and felt her hand quiver. 'What exactly are the vows?'

'The ones I'll take next week? Chastity, primarily, then abstinence. I'll give up meat and probably alcohol, too.'

'But why?'

'Why not?'

She was tempted to ask if he knew what he'd be missing. 'Haven't you ever wanted to get married?'

'No. The idea appeals, of course, like the ideas of eating and drinking, but just because appetites exist doesn't make it necessary to feed them.'

'OK. So you won't starve without alcohol, and vegetarians can be healthy, but just how long can you do without sex?'

He took a hasty mouthful of wine. 'I'm still a virgin actually.'

It was Domina who blushed.

'Well . . . Oh God . . . I suppose one can't say wait until you're not before you give it up,' she said. 'Quintus, it's only that I hate that kind of finality. It's like the castrati. There's something immoral about asking a twelve-year-old choirboy, whose head is only full of Allegri, bells and smells, whether he minds awfully giving his balls to Jesus.'

'I'm not twelve.'

'No, but you are a virgin.' There was a pause while she poured out the last of the wine. Wish, she thought, as she gave herself the last drops. 'Are you really?'

'Yes.'

She watched her wine for a moment, swirling it in the bottom of the glass.

'Has Seb, I mean Brother Jerome, told you he was at Cambridge with me?'

'No.'

'Well, he was. We were in the same year. He came to my twenty-first birthday party.'

'I wonder why he's never mentioned it. He doesn't talk

about his past much. I haven't told him you're here, actually.'

'I think I can tell . . .'

'Domina, please . . .'

'I think I *ought* to tell you why.'

Quintus set aside his glass and started to stand. His knees had gone stiff and he had some difficulty.

'I'm sorry,' he said, 'I think you're going to say something malicious, and I'd rather not hear it. Thank you for . . .'

'Sit down.' She was encouraged by the firmness of her own voice in the sordid little room. She stared up at him until his gaze, gingerly, crept round to meet her own. 'Quintus, sit down.'

Slowly he lowered himself back to the floor. Still by the bed, but closer to the armchair now. When he spoke, his voice was uneven as a thirteen-year-old's.

'Well, tell me and then I think I should go back to my room and let you . . .' In crossing his legs, he kicked over the bowl of walnuts. They scattered across the carpet. 'Oh sorry,' he stuttered, reaching out an ineffectual hand.

'Never mind them. Now listen. I was at university with your Brother Jerome when he was still called Seb Saunders and was a notorious homosexual.'

'No. He . . .'

'He was witty, intelligent, vociferously irreligious, and quite open about his taste in men. He liked them tall, pale and thin. He'd have liked you.'

'Well, that was then. When he converted and took his vows he left all that behind him. I expect he prays for atonement every day.'

'But don't you see he's living a lie? When he took the vows of chastity, he lied. I know enough about Christianity to know about sinning in thought as well as deed, and I can't believe Seb changed his spots to that extent. I simply don't think you should be taking him as your spiritual guide. I've nothing against homosexuality – I expect you're more severe about it than I am – but I do think you should talk to someone of more, well, of more integrity before you take any vows.'

'You don't know Jerome. He's probably a changed man.'

'Your spiritual father drove a young cousin of mine to suicide.'

'No. You're just saying that.'

'He seduced him, made him fall in love with him, then threatened to wreck his career, and Gregory killed himself. Seb was only your age at the time; if he was like that then, I can only think he's worse now.'

As she talked, Quintus had been struggling, trying to leave, trying not to hear, but she had seen the earlier hesitation, she knew his Achilles' heel. Now he sat hunched against the bed staring down at the carpet. By the light of the candles she could see the glistening in his sea-green eyes. Secure in the knowledge that he was not now going to run away, she fell silent and waited, watching. After a moment he pushed the hair off his forehead and she saw that he was biting the inside of his lips. The time was right. She counted to ten, staring at the tremors of the skin below his mouth, and the clenching and pinching of his fingers in his lap. When she spoke, she made her voice as motherly as possible.

'Oh Quin, I'm so sorry. Perhaps I . . .' She waited for

him to look up, despair in his eyes, then held out her arms. 'Come here.'

With a sound approaching a yelp he half crawled, half fell across the small stretch of carpet between them and held her tight, his sobbing face in her breasts. She held one hand firmly against his shoulder blades and stroked his soft hair with the other, gazing at his long legs, laid so awkwardly out behind him, and murmuring, 'There there, you poor sweet fool. There there. It'll be all right. Everything'll be all right.'

As his sobbing grew less convulsive, she could make out the words, 'I can't bear it, I can't bear it.' The vibrations of his voice reached her ribs and made her shudder. She continued to stroke his hair and smiled down at him. His tears were beginning to wet her blouse. She could feel their hot wetness. She bent her head forward and sank her lips onto his crown with a low hum.

'There there,' she whispered, and kissed his hair again. It smelt of green apple shampoo and was as fine as a child's. Slowly, as she knew would happen, the weeping stopped and his embrace grew more controlled, more searching. As she felt one of his hands travel gradually up her spine, she bent her face towards him in readiness. As he raised his own, tear-stained, she pressed a kiss onto his blood-stiffened lips.

The struggle was minimal, a token gesture. Her first virgin, he barely fumbled at all. She was faintly disappointed at the accuracy of his intuitive moves. After she had blown out the candles and taken him into her bed, after she had worked out her several angers, at Gerald, at Seb, at Randy's infidelity, and at this young man's sanctimonious self-negation, she was shocked that the lovemaking had been so pleasurable. In the final analysis her impulse had been a charitable one.

She found the matches and lit the candle she had left on the bedside table. She looked down on that face, attractive, only in a hopeless, ascetic way, of course. She smiled. He shut his eyes and sighed. In a darting movement, she took another fierce kiss from his mouth. Then she pulled back and her face was triumphant.

'Go on,' she murmured, 'go on, Quin, say it again.'

The expression in his eyes was untroubled, empty.

'You're the Boss,' he said, 'no one else can do this but you 'cause you're the Boss.'

'Good boy.' She blew out the candle.

23

Domina was typing out a third act. It was inhumanely hot. She had a carton of pineapple juice on the table beside Ray and paused to take a swig from time to time, or to mop the sweat from her face and arms with a large red handkerchief. Even in these pauses her concentration did not lapse, her eyes remained on the emerging page. The telephone rang occasionally and she would ignore it. At one stage, a hand rapped smartly on her door and Mr Punjabi called out.

'Mrs Tey? Excuse me. Mrs Tey, are you there?'

She only fell silent and kept still until his steps descended the stairs once more, her eyes fixed on her work. Her alarm clock had run down, but she must have worked solidly for over five hours.

She had slept a sound and dreamless sleep. She had woken when Quintus climbed out of bed. She opened her eyes to see him pulling on his trousers. He saw her wake and smiled, putting a finger to his lips.

'Ssh. Go back to sleep. I'm just going to make a phone call. Back in a sec.'

Only half awake in any case, she had fallen fast asleep again, holding last night's scenario at a mental arm's length as unfit for too immediate a scrutiny. She had woken later to the smell of fresh coffee. He had brought her up a tray: coffee, a *petit pain au chocolat* and a glass of orange juice.

'Hello,' he said, and kissed her lightly on the forehead.

'Angel,' she murmured, and sat up to drain the sleep from her skull. She took the glass in both hands and sipped some juice, while he stared at her. He seemed to have tidied the room. At the moment, the only thing she could register was confusion. She was at a loss as to how she should be feeling. 'Who did you telephone?'

'How would you like to fly to the Isle of Wight for a picnic?'

'Quintus, this is most unlike you.'

'Don't tease. Well? Would you come?'

'I'd love to. But it isn't a Sunday.'

'That's OK. I rang Brian and he said no one's booked the Chipmunk all day. It's all ours. Do you have to work?'

'Well, no,' she laughed, uncertainly. 'But what about you? Surely . . . er . . . church?'

'I said don't tease. Hurry up and eat your breakfast and we'll be off. I've put some petrol in the car.'

'Is there an airport on the Isle of Wight?'

'Of course. Not a big one, but it's there. You used to be able to fly over from near Portsmouth. Shall I run you a bath?'

'Please,' she said without thinking, and he was gone.

When she determined to seduce him, Domina had spared no thought to the morning, indeed the mornings, after. There had been a blind, single-minded fury, then a glowing sense of victory that was somehow philanthropic, then she had fallen asleep. Did she love him? Surely not – Randy was the one she loved. Did Quin love her? Presumably he was bound to be fairly infatuated, she being his number one and so forth. As she bathed, as she dressed, as she was bounced in the Morris beside him, Domina was amused and mildly alarmed that she was being presented with a romantic dilemma. Quintus was undoubtedly attractive, albeit only in an ascetic way. He had even proved potentially good in bed. Having taken it upon herself to rescue him from a living death, she couldn't simply wave bye-bye.

There again she was almost twice his age. She found herself cast in a role that was at once maternal, sexual and vaguely divine. By the time they drew up in the car park at Biggin Hill, she had decided that it was not a part she wanted to play. They would have a lovely time at the Isle of Wight, then she would firmly, kindly, get the hell out of Bayswater. He was bright. He would survive. Perhaps she would let him make love to her once more before she left – for the memory's sake.

They had bought a picnic in Notting Hill before setting off. Together they carried the bags and rugs over to the tiny, waiting craft. They loaded it up, then Domina stood below, watching, while the same technician finished whatever it was he did with the engine. He had just finished when Quintus turned to speak.

'Domina, could you do me a huge favour?'

'Yes. What?'

'I've just remembered I'd arranged to have lunch with Brother Jerome.'

'Do you want me to ring him and pretend to be Tilly or something?'

'Could you?'

'Of course. What's the number?'

'Damn. I can't remember it offhand. It's in my address

book in the glove compartment. Here, I'll give you the keys. There's a pay-phone on the stairs to the spectators' gallery.'

'OK. I'll tell the old bugger you've had to go home urgently.'

'No. Just say that I can't come. That's all I'd have told Tilly.'

She walked back to the car and found the number. Then she climbed the staircase and found a pay-phone by the doors which led out onto the rooftop. She dialled the number. A man's voice answered.

'Hello?'

'Is that Brother Jerome?' she asked, knowing it wasn't.

'No. I'm afraid he's out at the moment. Can I take a message?'

'Yes, please. Could you tell him that Quintus Harding can't come for lunch today after all.'

'He can't?'

'No. He's gone flying. Could you tell him that? It would be so kind.'

'All right.'

'Thank you.'

'Goodbye.'

''Bye.'

As she turned from the telephone, Domina saw the Chipmunk through the windows in the door. It was coasting out onto the runway. She ran out onto the terrace, to the far corner and waved frantically.

'Quin! Hang on! I'm just coming.'

Then it had stopped. One of the doors opened and he leaned out and waved to her. Even at that distance she had been able to see that he was smiling. She laughed, assuming he was going to wait for her out there, then stopped as she saw him swing the aeroplane onto the runway and accelerate it.

Alone on the gravelled roof she leaned on the railings. The white Chipmunk climbed steeply after leaving the ground, and veered off to the left. As she watched, Domina realized that Quin was travelling in a wide circle about the airfield, a circle that spiralled upwards. He was showing off to her. She giggled aloud, wondering what his mother would think. She waved as he passed overhead. Her smile cut as she heard the sound of the engine die.

He was not as high as they had been on Sunday. She watched as the craft glided on for perhaps ten or fifteen seconds on its course, then, after seeming to hang motionless in the air for an instant, fell in silence to the runway. It was like watching a film of his death with the soundtrack muted. The noise of the flimsy vessel plummeting nose first on to the tarmac and bursting into flames seemed to come from a distant field.

The tail-end was already buckling down into the billowing blackness when the pocket-sized fire engine trundled out. Domina's sense of exclusion was accentuated by the initial silence of its approach. Somewhere in the building beneath her, a huge metal door rolled back, then the vehicle appeared. Two men in black uniform were clinging to its gleaming red side and a light was spinning blue-white, blue-white on top of the cab. The bell only coughed into life moments before the men leapt down. It jangled for a few seconds, then ceased as apologetically as it had begun. As they unwound a hose and started to douse the flames, a third man, in a silvery suit with gloves and helmet to match, jumped from the cab and ran, a kitchen-foil bee-keeper, into the conflagration. Frozen at her railing, Domina saw men appearing from different corners of the aerodrome. They gathered at some distance, standing with their hands at their sides. As a breeze brushed some of the smoke in their direction she made out a sound of coughing. A few handkerchiefs flapped.

A siren wailed across the car park and a family saloon painted white, with AMBULANCE on the doors, rushed in a wide circle around the scene, coming to rest on the far side. A man and a woman climbed out. She carried a blanket over one arm and leaned against the bonnet coughing, while her colleague pulled out a stretcher. For the first time Domina noticed the quiet similarity between a Volvo and a hearse.

There was a house to her left, a small 1940s place. A boy in a red jersey and a girl in a blue had clambered onto the garden fence and were shouting incoherently, banging their sandalled feet on the wood below them. See John. See the red fire engine! See Janet climb the fence! Dog Rover hear the bells!

The flames were dying down but the smoke, steam perhaps, had doubled in volume. A puddle was forming, incongruous, around the pyre. As the man in silver emerged, the crowd of men shifted forward slightly. One of them turned and ran back into the building beneath her feet. A woman called sharply from the door of the little house. The girl in blue slipped over the fence and ran back to join her. They vanished. The boy remained, still swinging his legs. Something had been dragged from the steaming wreckage and the woman by the bonnet was covering it with her blanket. She was not coughing now.

As the family saloon sped, wailing, to the exit gates, Domina returned to the waiting Morris. She found she was still clutching the keys. She unlocked the driver's door and sat in his seat, then noticed the gaping glove compartment. The address book was still by the pay-phone. She climbed back up to retrieve it before driving off.

Domina held together the sheets she had typed and tapped them into a neat block which she then stapled together at the margin. Only a first draft, but it was all there. The ending was particularly strong: a Cowardly dénouement in which Fay Harker and Barnaby, her young priest, were confronted *in flagrante delicto* by draconian mother, sundry clergymen, lodgers, landlady etc. and brazened it out. There was no curtain line yet, but that she traditionally left until rehearsals were under way. She paused as she prepared to slide the work into an envelope for Des, and reached for the Tipp-Ex. She covered the old title, *Taking Rides* and replaced it with *Maiden Voyage*. She sealed the new-born play into the envelope. Then she stood looking out of the window over the rooftops to the red insanity of the Coburg Hotel roof. She ran her fingers through her hair, yawned and stretched. It was time to go home.

24

'We'll be ever so sorry to see you leave,' said Tilly, 'won't we, Tel?'

'She'll be back, Madame,' Thierry pronounced.

Domina was clearing her shelf in the larder. The news of Quintus's death was still filtering through the house. Two policemen had called last night. She offered herself as a witness, and they had taken her statement. They sat on Tilly's sofa, while the mistress retired tactfully with Grace to the bedroom, and she told them how Quintus had driven her to the aerodrome that morning. She said that she had felt sick on her first trip with him, and so had agreed to stay on the ground and watch. It was clearly an accident and she was sorry not to have contacted them at once, she said, but she had driven home in a state of understandable shock. They had seemed satisfied.

Domina supposed that her numbness, her utter lack of emotion even now that a dreamless night had passed, was also a symptom of shock. Dispassionately, she watched Tilly, Avril and Thierry in turn edge around her impending grief, raising any topic but the one on all their minds. Dispassionately, she wondered when the calm was going to crack.

'So you've found somewhere to live?' Thierry asked, when Tilly had gone out.

'Yes,' she said. 'It's absolutely perfect. Only fifty

minutes from Paddington, so you must come and see me one day.'

'But where? Not London?'

'No. A very little, rather quiet place called Clifton.'

She left her carrier bagful of groceries with her luggage in the hall. Randy had said he'd be here by twelve-thirty. It was so like him to ask no questions. No 'Hi, how're you doing?', no 'What's up?', no 'Just give me a couple of hours to finish off here'. He had simply said, 'I'll be with you around half of twelve. Give me the address.'

She walked to Queensway to post the new manuscript to Des, then walked up to Kensington Gardens to wait for her man. She had told Tilly where he could find her. She couldn't stand another minute in that house.

The weather was kindly fickle; the day cloudy without being humid. A few tourists, sated with sights, had left their hotels for a jog under the trees. Domina struck off along the wide path that ran parallel to the Bayswater Road towards Lancaster Gate. She had not yet decided how much she would tell Randy – certainly not all. Just Gerald, perhaps, in fair return for Cary. Packing her bags had had a comforting, last day of school air. Knowing that Randy was on his way to collect her made Domina feel safe. She had been a big, brave girl quite long enough.

The Italian Garden was close now. She could hear the splashing of water and make out the absurd stone pavilion between the trees. A large dog, like an Alsatian, only black, bounded across the path in front of her, snatched up a fat stick, then galloped back to the right, up the gentle slope. In the clearing there a little girl was trying to fly her kite. A man held it aloft while, several feet away, she grasped the string.

'Now run. Run!' he shouted. Whimpering, she ran away, string held up in a fist. He let go. There was a little wind and her legs were short, so the toy swung round a few times, then slammed into the turf.

'Stop or you'll break it!' he yelled. 'Stop!'

Domina walked past the thigh-high wall into the water garden. Only two fountains were working properly. The others, broken or clogged with feathers and fish scales, merely seeped. Staring down at the ducks as they fought over bread or sat preening on their wooden ramps, she followed the perimeter and came to lean against the balustrade over the 'source' of the Serpentine. The roaring of traffic impinged on the scene. It was a lunch-break place – pretty enough, and convenient for buses, but hopelessly urban. Embarrassed by the cameras clicking around her, she returned to the path and followed the Serpentine.

Suddenly there was barking close beside her. She turned and saw the dog again. Ham. No, Japhet. He ran up, wagging his tail, and tried to jump up.

'Hello,' she said and stooped to rub his chest. He sat, panting, staring up at her. Someone called further along the path, 'Japh. Here boy. Come here!' It was a man in a well-tailored black suit. He had on a black tie and had shaved his head. 'Here! Japhet!'

The dog bounded over to him and sat while his master fastened on a leash. When the man straightened up and began to walk towards her, Domina recognized Brother Jerome. Seb Saunders. He had taken a razor to his scalp.

Her immediate impulse was to hurry away into the crowd; she could wait for Randy on the porch. There was no need to meet the man. Then she thought of Quintus. She thought of his disbelief when she'd told him of his mentor's history. She was walking towards him. Trying to find the right words, she raised a half smile in readiness. She saw the blood clots on his skin where the razor had slipped. He was close now. Then she couldn't bear it. Raising a wave and a smile to a man who wasn't there, she started to run and called out to the middle distance.

'Jamie, hi! Wait for me!'

She was in flat shoes and managed to run a hundred yards before she lost her breath. Ashamed and awkward, she dropped into a bench beside some willows on the water's edge. By degrees her panting slowed. She took out a handkerchief and dried her palms. Some geese were sifting the small, tame waves. She studied them hard in an effort to calm herself.

'You should have been clutching a red carnation, Mrs Tey.'

It was Randy. He sat down beside her and they fell into an ungainly side-saddle embrace.

'Good to see you,' he said over her shoulder.

'God, it's good to see you too,' she gasped and started to cry. He didn't notice at first, but with the first sob he straightened up slightly and tried to stroke her face.

'Hey there. Steady on,' he said with a grin. But she buried her face in his shirt, grinding her cheek on a button, needing to feel hurt. She tried to stop, but her throat constricted painfully. She had to release more wrenched sobs to relieve the burn. With Randy to hold her she was being drawn out of shock, of course. These were tears for Quintus.

'I'm crying for Quin,' she sought to tell herself, 'I'm crying for Quin. This is right and healthy and to be expected.'

But as the convulsions subsided and she dared to raise her eyes over Randy's shoulder to the statue of Peter Pan behind him, she realized that she was weeping with rage because she couldn't understand. The secular Jermyn Street suit and tie and the outraged scalp had lain beyond the compass of her ready wits. She was left frustrated, imperceptive, ugly.

As Randy wiped her eyes, helped her blow her nose and walked her in tender silence to his car, it occurred to Domina for the first time in two days that she might be with child. Sleeping that night in his all-American arms, she relived in merciless detail a visit to some poky rooms in Ipswich, and murdered a second baby to the wails of plummeting aircraft.

25

The three of them were in evening dress. Rick had flopped, spent, into an armchair. Ginny had kicked off her tight best shoes and had slung her legs up on the sofa. Only the Milanese standard lamp was on, casting a fan of bluish light up one wall. The ugly, gold-plated trophy had been placed, for the nonce, on the mantelpiece. Randy had discarded his dinner jacket and undone his black tie.

'Brandy, Ginny?' he asked, at the sideboard.

'Rather.'

'Night-cap, Rick?'

'Please, Randy.'

Domina appeared from the basement stairs. She was yawning.

'All well?' Ginny called from the sofa.

'Ssh,' Rick said. 'You'll wake little one.'

'Yes. All's fine,' Domina sighed.

'Darling?'

'Bless you.' She took the glass which Randy held out for her, and sank onto the arm of Rick's chair, smiling down at his round, solicitous face. 'Cary and Seamus say she's been as good as gold. They fed her three hours ago and Cary changed her nappies and not a murmur since.'

'I'll take them a drink,' said Randy. 'Are they still in the kitchen?'

'No.' She stopped him. 'They've gone to bed.'

'Seamus is a reformed character since young McNichol moved in with him,' said Rick.

'And it must be such a help having her handy around the house,' added his wife, looking nowhere in particular.

'I'm a walking corpse,' said Domina, ignoring her.

'Yes, you must be.' Rick made as if to rise. 'Ginny, we mustn't stay. Nursing mothers should be in bed.'

'No, honestly.' Domina laid a stilling hand on his shoulder. 'Don't rush off. It's good to unwind. I do think it was unnecessary of that newsreader cow to draw attention to my recent condition. I wasn't feeling especially glam as it was, and having her broadcast my stretch marks to the nation like that was the end.'

'She didn't exactly . . .'

'Oh yes. I know. But she did make it sound as if I'd literally crawled in from the labour ward.'

'Well, bravo anyway,' said Randy.

'Thanks.'

'Yes, bravo that author.'

'Well, bravo you too, Ginn. It was your production, after all.'

'Hardly. Fi is great though. It's the first time she's actually deserved an award *before* getting it, usually it's the other way around.'

'I liked your Bayswater discovery, darling. What's her name? The floozy in the second scene.'

'Penny Havers? Good, isn't she?'

'So natural,' added Ginny, swigging the last of her drink.

'What were you and Des talking about, Rick?' asked Domina. 'You were nose to nose.'

'Oh. Dear Des. She was full of her book.'

'Des writing a book at long last?' asked Randy.

'No, not *hers* – the one she's handling for some old trout. Sounds fascinating. It started life as a ghosted auto-biography, then Des persuaded her that the fictionalized bits were so good, she might as well fictionalize the whole thing and pass it off as her own.'

'What's it about?'

'Some astonishing tale of perversion and matricide in the sixties underworld.'

'You know Des is dying of something?'

'Ginny, are you serious?'

'Oh yes. Poor Dan Nixon says they meet regularly in the queue on chemotherapy days.'

Domina opened her mouth to exclaim, but was distracted by a thin jerky wail from above.

'I hear a little voice,' said Rick.

'Duty calls.'

'No, Minnie, I'll go,' said Randy, rising, 'it's my turn.'

'Are you sure?'

'Yup. You stay put.'

'Who's sweet?'

'Daddy-o.'

Randy gave Domina's proffered hand a squeeze and went to quiet the baby's cries.

'Does she still cry a lot?' asked Virginia.

'Not much, but she gets nightmares. She's that age. Never a whimper during the day. Big and brave.'

'Like Daddy, eh?'

'Ginny, we must be off.' Rick stood up and held out a hand to his wife. He hauled her from the chair.

'Oh, you big bully,' she muttered. 'All right. You get the

coats while I say 'night 'night to our heroine.' Rick left the room. Ginny gave Domina a wavering kiss on the cheek, then stood back holding her hands. 'I'm so glad she turned out, well, you know . . . all right. We worried for you.'

'The forty-year miracle, eh?'

'Who *is* the father, darling?'

Domina grinned and murmured, 'She smiled her enigmatic smile and said, "M.Y.O.B".'

'Beast. I think it was Randy all along, and you're just trying to make me jealous.'

'Me? Never. Goodnight, Rick darling.'

'Night.'

'Goodnight, you.' She kissed Ginny again.

When they were gone, she turned out the lights and started up the stairs. They had made the nursery in her old study, across the landing from the bedroom, and she had moved her things up to the attics that were still in mid-conversion. She paused on the landing to take stock of herself in the wide gilt mirror. Last time it had been Best Comedy, tonight she had graduated to Best Play. A comedy with a soul, they had called it. She ran her nails through her hair. It needed a cut. This time she would leave the grey hairs untouched – Randy's had started and looked so distinguished. Tomorrow she would start work in earnest on the revisions of *She the Rover*, a study of a Restoration woman playwright and her bisexual husband, loosely based on the marriage of Aphra Behn.

She saw the reflection of Randy's legs coming out of the nursery and standing above her on the main landing.

'Quit preening, Mouse, and come up here.'

She stayed where she was, smiling up at his warm, tanned face. North Africa had done him a power of good.

'How is she?'

'Our little Magdalen's sleeping sound.' He started down the stairs and sat just above her with a knee on either side of her shoulders.

'Don't pronounce it like that, she's not an Oxford college. For that matter, she doesn't *have* to be Oxbridge material.'

'Oh no?' He bent forward and nuzzled into her neck, his long arms drawing her back against his chest. She kissed him on the temple.

'I love you, Pluto,' she said and looked forward to where he was smiling at her from out of the looking glass. Tonight she would ask him to marry her.

A PLACE CALLED WINTER
Patrick Gale

Harry Cane has followed tradition at every step, until an illicit affair forces him to abandon the golden suburbs of Edwardian England and travel to the town of Winter in the newly colonised Canadian prairies. There, isolated in a beautiful but harsh landscape, Harry embarks on an extraordinary journey, not only of physical hardship, but also of acute self-discovery.

'Gale's confident, supple prose expresses the labour and hardship that toughen Harry's body as they calm his mind . . . Harry Cane is one of many, the disappeared who were not wanted by their families or their societies and whose stories were long shrouded with shame. This fascinating novel is their elegy' *Guardian*

'Gale's novels are imbued with clear-eyed psychological truths navigating the emotional landscape of characters it is impossible not to care about deeply. Sensitive and compelling' *Irish Times*

'A mesmerising storyteller; this novel is written with intelligence and warmth' *The Times*

TINDER
PRESS

ISBN 978 1 4722 0531 5

A PERFECTLY GOOD MAN
Patrick Gale

'A writer with heart, soul, and a dark and naughty wit, one whose company you relish and trust' *Observer*

On a clear, crisp summer's day in Cornwall, a young man carefully prepares to take his own life, and asks family friend, John Barnaby, to pray with him. Barnaby – priest, husband and father – has always tried to do good, though life hasn't always been rosy. Lenny's request poses problems, not just for Barnaby, but for his wife and family, and the wider community, as the secrets of the past push themselves forcefully into the present for all to see.

'This being Gale there's a compelling tale to be told . . . a convincing, moving account of man's struggle with faith, marriage and morality' *Sunday Times*

'A thoughtful and moving novel about love, morality and faith. Marvellous' *Mail on Sunday*

'A heartfelt, cleverly constructed read' *Independent on Sunday*

TINDER
PRESS

ISBN 978 1 4722 5542 6

ROUGH MUSIC
Patrick Gale

'Sparkling with emotional intelligence. A gripping portrait of a marriage and quiet, devastating fall-out of family life' *Independent*

Julian is a contented if naïve only child, and a holiday on the coast of North Cornwall should be perfect, especially when distant American cousins join the party. But their arrival brings upheaval and unexpected turmoil.

It is only as a seemingly well-adjusted adult that Julian is able to reflect on the realities of his parents' marriage, and to recognise that the happy, cheerful boyhood he thought was his is infused with secrets, loss and the memory of betrayals that have shaped his life.

'A subtle, highly evocative tale of memory and desire' *Mail on Sunday*

'Like the sea he describes so well, Patrick Gale's clear, unforced prose sucks one in effortlessly' Elizabeth Buchan, *Daily Mail*

'A painfully acute but never reproachful examination of a past that will not vanish' *Daily Telegraph*

TINDER
PRESS

ISBN 978 1 4722 5540 2

You are invited to join us behind the scenes at Tinder Press

TINDER
PRESS

To meet our authors, browse our books
and discover exclusive content on our
blog visit us at

www.tinderpress.co.uk

For the latest news and views from the team
Follow us on Twitter

 @TinderPress